DON'T WHISPER IN MY EAR

DON'T WHISPER IN MY EAR

Sandy Dal Santo

Lake House Publishing
Fountain Hills, Arizona
sdalsanto.lakehousepublishing@gmail.com

Printed in the United States of America

ISBN 978-1-7354961-1-5
ISBN 978-1-7354961-0-8

First printed August 2020

TABLE OF CONTENTS

ONE

Chicago, September 1979

A Capricorn will never forget a sin

Many years ago my mother told me only weak people cried. From then on, I refused to show weakness. When I was younger, my tears weren't intimidated by my mother's words, so they rolled down my cheeks often when I cried alone in my room.

Last January, I turned seventeen. I was one year older than the age my mother's life was shattered, and now it was my turn. When I got home from school, my mother was on the phone with her back to me. I couldn't tell who she was talking to, but her tone didn't sound friendly. Waiting for her to hang up, I dropped my backpack on the dining room table and searched for my lip gloss before peering into the large mirror hanging above where a piano used to be. The sunlight shining into the dining room window captured my sea-green eyes in the mirror. Only two percent of the population had green eyes. This made me unique and a little special. If only I could get others to see that, especially Mom. It was complicated.

"She's home now. I'll talk to you later."

Mom's eyes were blue, but not sapphire blue, more like sky blue. Looking into my mom's eyes, was like looking into a deep hole that never ended. The distance between the sky and the sea was the same distance my mother and I had between us. Even though blue eyes were pretty, I preferred mine to be sea green.

Mom and I shared the same dirty blonde hair color, and many people said we look alike, but I didn't want to be like her at all.

"Why are you home so early?" I asked.

"I quit my job, and I'm moving to Breckenridge, Colorado…" She was leaving, and she didn't mention me. My heart sank realizing she didn't even care if I didn't come with her. I wasn't surprised. I'd always felt one day she would leave. I just didn't know when. But I wasn't going to let her leave me—not yet. There were too many things I needed to learn about her and myself.

My mother worked as a secretary at a company in town. For ten years she dated the boss's son, who was several years younger than her. And now she didn't have a job. I wondered what happened at work or with her boyfriend. Did they have a fight? Did they break up? Or did she type something wrong at work? Was either of these the reason she had quit her job?

She brushed her breakfast crumbs from the table onto the carpet. I watched them fall.

Damn it, I just vacuumed yesterday.

I crossed my arms over my chest to block her words from hurting me. I knew what was coming. "And what am I supposed to do?"

Without looking at me she said, "You can stay here, or you can come with me."

I didn't think she really wanted me to go with her or she would have said it in a different way, like. "I quit my job. Let's run away to Breckenridge, just the two of us. It will be fun." But she didn't.

"Are you serious Mom? This is my senior year. How can you ask me to quit school and leave with you? I'm supposed to graduate this year! What about my friends? And where will we live?"

"It's your decision to stay or go. I'm leaving in the morning," she said, walking toward her bedroom. I followed her down the dark hallway and stopped in front of her room. She packed her suitcase in an organized calm.

"Why—"

"If you're coming, you need to start packing now!"

"So, if I don't go with you, you're just going to leave me here by myself? I'm only seventeen. Can I even live by myself?"

I can't live on my own. I don't know how. I'm only seventeen.

She didn't answer.

I retreated to my room, sat on my bed, and stared down the hallway. I rubbed at my aching temples. A tear dropped from each eye as my chest started to heave. I jumped off my bed and slammed the door.

After dinner I went to the backyard, my playground when I was younger. I played baseball and built a wooden fort behind the garage with my friends. Where I had my first kiss with the boy next door. In the winter, we froze the yard and made a hockey rink. I fought with my sister over who would cut the grass. Outside the back door was where we kept the kegs of beer wrapped in a blanket. I had the coolest and classiest parties of anyone in high school. My house was "the place to be." Old wine bottles covered in layered wax drippings of red, blue, and green sat on most tables. Many candlelit hours were spent drinking and partying with friends, and where the scent of incense masked the smell of anything illegal being smoked inside. A ping-pong table in the basement tested the athletic abilities of my friends, who were not very athletic at all. And, of course, this was the house where I crashed my mom's car into the back of our garage, as I tried to park after drinking all night.

Every summer, my grandpa planted a garden of tomatoes, pole beans, cabbage, carrots, and lettuce behind our garage. He also had a garden at their house where he grew radishes, tomatoes, bell peppers (which her neighbors helped themselves to regularly), Kohlrabi, strawberries, and grapes.

My mother didn't like strawberries, but it didn't stop my grandmother from making strawberry jam or strawberry shortcake for dessert. She also made cinnamon applesauce. While the apples were cooking, she'd throw in some cinnamon candies turning the apple sauce a pretty pink color and making it a little sweeter. On weekends when my mom and I visited, I would creep down the stairs to the cold, dark basement and pull jars of grape and strawberry jelly from the shelves along with the jars of apple sauce and stewed tomatoes. I was leaving all this behind. I hoped it was worth it.

The next morning Mom pounded on my bedroom door and woke me. "Now, Sandra Kay Kelly, I'm leaving now!"

I threw back the covers and sat up. The sun blinded me as I grabbed my jeans and yanked them on. My suitcase was packed, but I had left it open just in case I had more to put inside. I had to rush because I knew she would leave without me.

Why was she doing this?

The acid from my stomach burned the back of my throat when I bent over to zip my suitcase up. She pounded on the door again.

“Now,” she said.

“I’m coming. Can I at least brush my teeth? I’m sure you don’t want to smell my breath all the way there. Give me one minute.”

Please don’t leave without me. I don’t want you to leave me.

I took one last look around my room, pushing back the tears I wished I could control. Before I left, I closed the curtains on the window I used to crawl through to run away into the night with my friends after Mom and I fought. She’d tell me, "Smoke a joint or go to your room." I never won those arguments with my mother, so I lived in my room or ran away.

I opened my closet door to see if I had all the clothes I wanted. I thought about the time I hid in the back when my mother told me my uncle died. I didn’t want diabetes to find me too. I was afraid I would die. I backed away from the closet and bumped into an empty birdcage, which fell onto my bed that wasn’t mine to begin with. Nothing was ever bought for me. Everything was always bought for someone else first.

I had called my dad the night before to see if I could stay with him. He said there was no room for me. My sister who was three years older had moved in with him last year. She got there first. I opened the top drawer of my dresser that my dad made for me when I was a baby. I ran my hand along the inside. I wished I could bring this with me, but there was no room in our car, like there was no room for me in his home. My stomach hurt so much it felt like it could explode. I saw my chalkboard where I kept track of all the guys I liked. Some had stars by their names and some didn't. I brushed my hand over their names. They disappeared in white dust forever. Maybe my grandma would store everything in her attic as she did for everyone in our family. I grabbed my suitcase off the bed, shut the light off and closed the bedroom door that someone else would have.

Widget, my cat was waiting in the hall. He was my bird's killer. He was never tried and convicted because my mother or sister left my bedroom door open. Though they both knew my parakeet was in there. One of them took that away from me. I got that bird for something to love. I wanted to hear it sing and fill my room with happiness. I found out later that birds don't sing because they're happy. They're happy because they sing. Just like we sing when we're happy.

Widget circled my legs like he always did in the morning. I brushed his golden fur with my hand and scratched his one and a half ears. "Goodbye, cat. Sharon will come get you. You'll be ok. Stay out of the street. I don't want anything to happen to you." I set my suitcase down, picked him up, and cradled him in my arms. "Can you keep a secret?" I whispered in his partially missing ear.

He rubbed his head back and forth against my hand.

"Good. I don't want to leave or leave you. But I can't stay. I have to go with mom. I need more time to make her love me, like you do." Widget purred and nuzzled his head into my neck. "I'm hoping everything will be better in Colorado. Maybe she'll change, or perhaps I'll change."

He nudged his chin against my finger and lightly nipped it. "Meow," was all he said.

The car horn honked. "I better go before she leaves me." I kissed his forehead and ran out the front door. "Geeze, mom, you'll wake the neighbors." I opened the car door and dropped my suitcase on the back seat. "I'm ready, I guess," I said, sliding into the front seat of my mom's 1974 Plymouth Duster. My grandma bought this house and my mom's car. She paid all the bills, and both my grandma and step-grandfather took care of it. My mother never owned anything or took care of anything, not even her children. Mom backed out of the driveway and drove away from our two-bedroom bungalow where we'd lived for the past eleven years. We drove past the 31 flavors ice cream shop. "Do you remember what happened there?" I asked, turning toward her.

She said nothing.

I remembered what happened. My mom stopped there on her way home after a date near closing time. An armed man rushed in ordering her and the employee behind the cooler at gunpoint. He cleaned out the cash register and left. After that incident, I was afraid one day she wouldn't come home. I didn't know why my mother was running, but maybe going with her and getting away from whatever made her so unhappy meant we could have a normal relationship. I wanted her to be happy, and I wanted to be loved.

Before we merged onto I80 West, I noticed she never looked back like I did. It was like she had already put that life behind her. I envied the way she could do that. I would love to be able to forget the parts of my life that I didn't like. If my mother could erase her trauma, then why couldn't I erase mine? I knew why. It was because for me, I was faced with it every day. In the halls, in my classes at school since the fifth grade. Even when he wasn't physically there, he was there in my thoughts. I couldn't escape him. The fact that no one else knew also haunted me. I knew no one would believe me, which was why I didn't tell. I would never tell. Perhaps moving away would help me put it behind me. Perhaps I could learn to not look back the same way my mother could. A shiver ran through my body and then a feeling of relief settled in.

"The map shows it will take 16 hours to get there. Are we going to stop somewhere or drive straight through?" I asked.

"We'll stop in Lincoln, Nebraska, where we stayed last year."

I pressed the radio dial turning it left and then right. All I could find was talk radio.

Why wasn't anything on?

"Stop playing with that. You'll break it." Mom shoved my hand away.

"How am I going to break it?" I glared at her.

"I'm sure you'll find a way." She pulled a cigarette out of her purse and lit it. The smoke billowed from between her lips and out the partially rolled down window.

"You shouldn't smoke anymore," I said, waving the smoke away from my face.

"Why do you care?" She asked.

"Because I don't want you to die."

If she didn't care about herself why should I? I guess I cared because if she did die, I'd be alone. Her lips puckered as she inhaled again. She blew the smoke and flicked the ashes out the window.

Fifteen hours and 40 minutes to Breckenridge.

The flat treeless prairies along Interstate 80 through western Illinois and Iowa were so boring. There were so many ranches and farmhouses with white wood fences that I couldn't tell where one started and the other ended. Different colored cattle lined both sides of the highway, and I smelled them all a mile away. Farmers harvested the last of their crops for the season. The wind kicked up the dry dirt and danced it around in circles until it blew away. The only sound was the heartbeat of the concrete beating beneath the car. I closed my eyes and reclined the back of my seat.

Our car shook, and I bolted up as a semi-truck roared by. I readjusted my seat back and sat up.

"If you get tired I can drive."

Without taking her eyes off the road, she said. "I don't think so."

"Why? I'm a good driver," I said.

"Really? Okay, then, tell me why there's a scratch and a dent on the front bumper?

"Uhm…"

"And how did the back of the garage get pushed back? Did you think I wouldn't notice?"

"I don't know what happened. Maybe Sharon did it," I said.

"So, you're blaming this on your sister? Nice try. She hasn't lived with us for over a year. And since you're the only one who lives in my house and has a set of my car keys, I thought you'd know," she said.

"Did you tell Sharon we were leaving?" I asked.

"She knows."

"Is she coming to get the cat?"

"I'm sure she will."

"Did you tell dad we were leaving?"

"Don't worry about it," she snapped.

"How will he know where to mail the child support check?"

"Did you tell your dad you were leaving?" She asked.

"Yes…I asked if I could move in with him."

"What did he say?"

"There wasn't enough room for me," I mumbled. I slid toward the door and rested my head on the window.

So, I guess there's room for a cat and not me?

Twelve hours to Breckenridge

The wind picked up in Nebraska, and the car swerved every time a gust blew across the highway. Dirt, paper and garbage swirled in the wind. Weathervanes spun around on top of barns like plane propellers getting ready for takeoff.

After three hours of being trapped together in the car, I thought my mother would finally tell me what was really going on and I could fix her.

"So, now will you tell me why you quit your job? And why you had to leave?"

"You don't need to know." Mom pulled another cigarette out, lit it and puffed away.

I pressed my lips into a line. I guess the only time she talked was when I pissed her off.

"Where are you going to buy your pot when we get to Breckenridge?" I asked. "Or did you bring some with you?"

Mom didn't respond.

"Tell me again why you only had one pair of shoes when you were my age," I said.

"You and Sharon had everything you needed."

"No, we didn't. We needed you to be a mother, and you were never home. You were always gone." I dug my fingernails into my arm.

"You're old enough to take care of yourself," she lectured.

"Yeah, but I wasn't old enough when I was ten, and you would leave for the weekend."

"Your sister was there. She was old enough to take care of you," she justified.

Oh my god! She just didn't get it—I was only ten

"That wasn't her job. Do you know she hates me because of that? Why can't you be like other moms?"

"If you don't like the way I'm raising you, you can leave anytime," Mom said.

"Other moms are home and make dinner and bake cookies." I reached for the radio dial again.

She slapped my hand away.

"We go out for dinner every night and can order whatever you want. If you wanted a home cooked dinner, you could have made it yourself."

I couldn't believe she was justifying never being home and not taking care of my sister and me. "No, I couldn't. We never had any food in the house, and what we did have was moldy. And our refrigerator was disgusting. Only a scientist who was discovering a new form of penicillin would have liked what was in our refrigerator. And all you did was leave money for Sharon and me to get our own dinner on the weekends."

"So, you would have preferred I stayed home every night and not have a life?"

There it was. Her life was more important than us. "Ah, aren't we part of your life? At least you could have cared about what I was doing or where I went or if I was okay. What if something happened to me? How could I find you? Is this the way grandma raised you?"

"I had to take care of myself when I was your age," she said.

"You had grandma," I said.

"Not after my dad died. I had to cook dinner and clean the house when my mother went back to work. My brothers, your uncles, didn't have to do anything! I was only sixteen."

"So, this is why you—"

"Stop talking," she demanded.

"Why can't you love me? What did I do wrong?" I begged. I reclined my seat again and hid from her words.

I was only ten.

Maybe I made a mistake coming with her, one day I'd find out. The clock on the dashboard indicated we had ten more hours to go. This was going to be a long, long drive. Maybe silence was really golden.

Two

Capricorns are uncomfortable in what they cannot see

The summer before, mom and I went to Colorado on vacation. We had reservations at hotels and day trips planned to Pikes Peak and Garden of the Gods. We toured the Coors Brewery in Golden. At the hotel in Golden, I met a tall dark-haired, handsome boy who was my age. His name was Scott, and he was from Illinois too. His dad was there on business, so he was alone during the day.

We were both alone, so we spent the time together. But my mom wasn't there on business. I had no idea where she was. For the two days and two nights mom and I stayed there Scott and I hung out together at the pool and in the fitness room. We kissed in the fitness room when no one was looking.

Eight hours to Breckenridge

At four p.m., we took the highway exit for Lincoln, Nebraska and exited on the frontage road toward our hotel.

"Isn't this the same hotel we stayed at last year when we drove to Colorado?"

"Yes, it is," Mom said, getting out of the car.

"I'm going to go to the pool after dinner," I told her.

And I'm sure you remember the bar.

"Why Breckenridge? Why don't we go somewhere warm? How about California?" I followed Mom to the front desk. "I thought you liked Breckenridge?"

I pushed my suitcase along the tile floor with my foot as we moved up in line to check-in. "Yeah, for a vacation. I never said I wanted to live there. Besides, I don't even know how to ski, and isn't that what everyone does there?"

"You'll learn if you want to."

After getting the room key, we took the elevator up to the second floor. I unlocked and opened the door to a dimly lit room with two beds. I tossed my suitcase on the one closest to the window and crawled over, pushing the black-out curtains back. Outside, there were a few cars and a truck with a horse trailer with no horses inside. I wondered what they did with the horses? I fell back onto my bed and listened to the cars and trucks humming down the highway in the distance.

"Clean up and let's get dinner. There's a diner next door," Mom said.

Twenty minutes later, we were headed to the diner. We ate here last year. It wasn't fancy but the food was good.

"What are you wearing?" Mom asked.

I ran my hands down my front. "A shirt…," I said.

"No, not that. What am I smelling?" Mom asked.

"It's perfume. Love's Baby Soft. Why?"

"I don't like it," Mom said.

"I don't like your cigarette smoke."

Her face twisted. I backed off.

"Why can't you be a normal child?"

"Because I'm not a child," I said.

"Table for two?" the hostess asked.

"Yes," Mom answered.

The hostess seated us in a booth at the end of the aisle. There were only a few other people eating at another table. Several men sat at the counter talking and laughing, drinking coffee and eating pie. They were all dressed alike... Flannel shirts, jeans, boots. Some of the men wore cowboy hats and others wore ballcaps advertising oil companies. The scent of stale cigarette smoke and fresh brewed coffee hung in the air.

"You two must be sisters," the waitress said, pouring water for us.

"No, this is my mom."

"Well, Mom, you have a very pretty daughter."

I half smiled.

"Aren't you going to say thank you Sandy?" Mom directed.

"Thank you."

"No problem sweetie. What are you going to have for dinner?"

Holding the menu, I asked. "What is a buffalo burger?"

"It's a hamburger made with buffalo meat," the waitress said.

"Ewe. Uhm, I'll have a salad, and soup. What kind of soup do you have?"

"Split pea."

I wrinkled my nose. "Okay, I'll have a salad."

"Ma'am, what can I get you?"

"I'll have the liver and onions," Mom said.

Vomit rose into my mouth. "Uhm, can you make sure her liver and onions don't touch my salad?"

"You got it," the waitress said, walking away.

After dinner I went to the pool. It was indoors and I was the only one in there. I swam a few laps and cried under water. The water surrounding my body was like a hug. It was warm, and I liked the way it held me.

I had a choice to stay home or come with my mom and I wondered if I made the right choice. I leaned against the pool wall and imagined what I would be doing if I had stayed home. I'd either be at home with my friends playing an Aerosmith album with the TV on and the sound turned down, or at Holly's house trying on each other's clothes and gossiping about our friends. I didn't want to come with my mom, but I didn't want to be home alone either.

The door to the pool opened and a man with a gray shirt and pants entered carrying a mop and pulling a garbage can on wheels.

"Sorry, it's ten o'clock, the pool is closed," he said.

When I got back to our room Mom was in her bed playing solitaire. She didn't acknowledge me when I came in. I changed into my pajamas and climbed into bed with wet hair and the aroma of chlorine. I pulled my astrology book from my purse and started to read. I wanted to find out who I was.

Capricorns December 22 – January 19: The Goat

My birthday is January 18th. I am a Capricorn: A horned sea-goat, which is half goat, half fish. This must be why I have sea green eyes. And why am I a goat?

> Capricorns are organized, extremely responsible and tolerant.
>
> Capricorns are resourceful and talented people.
>
> When Capricorns find a target, they achieve it by hook or by crook.
>
> Capricorns are reliable friends.

Capricorns will not take risks without knowing the pros and cons. They are self-assured and have their feet rooted firmly on the ground.

Capricorns are extremely patient, and they're not impulsive. They will wait as long as required to analyze a situation before acting upon it.

Oh my God, this book was about me. So, this was why I was the way I was. I continued reading:

Capricorns see their lives in black and white. They tend to feel uncomfortable in what they can't see.

Astrologers define the Capricorn is a passive sign, but in reality, Capricorns are full of energy. When they put that energy into action they are assured of their success.

"Yep, try and stop me," I said aloud with determination.

I stared out the window through partially closed drapes at the streetlight. I wondered what my life would be like in Breckenridge. I hoped it would be different, I needed it to be better.

After breakfast we were back on the road again.

"How much longer until we get to Breckenridge," I asked.

"We should be there in nine more hours." Mom pulled a cigarette out of her purse.

I turned the radio on.

"You know there's nothing on this early."

Seven hours and 50 minutes to Breckenridge

"Do you remember in four months I'll be eighteen? It will be my golden birthday. I'll be 18 on the eighteenth. Are you going to plan something special for me? You'll have time to plan it."

She was silent.

"And your golden birthday was when you were eleven. Did you do anything special then? Did you go roller skating? Did grandma bake you a cake using salt instead of sugar? Like she did on my birthday last year?

She pulled another cigarette out of the pack and lit it. "You're old enough to plan your own party, and bake your own cake." Smoke trailed out of her mouth. She rolled the window down and blew the rest of the smoke out.

We drove through Hastings and North Platte, Nebraska, and soon entered Colorado. Off in the distance the Rocky Mountains exploded on the horizon. At first, I thought they were only clouds. I couldn't tell where the mountains ended and the sky began. Unpolluted white clouds blanketed the peaks. This was a drastic contrast to the Chicago smog. Up in the clouds I searched for something new: a new life in Breckenridge. It felt like heaven. While I didn't want to come here at first, this might be what I needed. God knew I was ready for it. I found a new love. Its name was Colorado.

"Mom, Mom?" She never answered. I rolled down my window and stuck my head out like a dog trying to catch air, but I was trying to catch my breath.

Four hours to Breckenridge

At three p.m., we pulled into the Holiday Inn parking lot in Dillon, fifteen short miles from Breckenridge.

"Do you know where we're going to live yet?" I asked.

"We'll find something in the morning. Why don't you go to the pool until it's dinner time?"

I got the hint: I was not needed in our room. I wish I had a window to crawl out of. Leaving through a window made me feel like I was escaping on my own terms. I changed into my swimsuit in front of the bathroom mirror. I glided my hand across my face and felt the smooth skin, searching for any imperfections. Then my eyes drifted lower. I swept my fingers across a three-inch scar above my right breast. Last year I found a lump. When I told my mother, she didn't believe me. She told me I was crazy—there was nothing there. I had to beg her to take me to the Doctor—I wanted him to tell me I was crazy— but he didn't. It wasn't cancerous, and other than this scar, there was nothing else wrong with me. But it didn't stop me from searching all the time. I was determined to find out why my mother treated me the way she did— maybe it was her. I left and headed for the pool.

After dinner we went back to the room. Mom sat on her bed, leaning over a newspaper and circling adds with a red pen.

"Find a place to work yet?" I asked searching for something to watch on TV.

"Not yet. I'll look for a job while you're at school. But I found an apartment right down the street from the high school. It sounds nice," she said.

"Thanks for thinking of me."

"I'm not doing it for you. If we lived farther away, I'd have to pay for a bus ticket."

Yeah, thanks again. At least you're honest.

Apartment for rent in Breckenridge:
Furnished 2 Bed 2 Bath Apartment for Rent
Immediate occupancy. Close to
shopping and Schools. Electric
and water included. Plenty of parking.

The next day we drove up to the brown brick apartment complex and met the landlord at the bottom of the iron and cement staircase. He took us to the first door at the top of the second floor and unlocked the two locks on the door.

"Here it is," he said.

He stood by the door while we went inside. It was a basic living room-- a couch, chairs, coffee tables, TV. The carpet was old but clean. I entered the living room and stepped out onto the balcony. The landlord joined me outside.

"Is that the ski mountain?" I asked.

"Yes, you have a view of the south run at Breckenridge."

"This is really nice. Mom?"

"She's down the hall," the landlord said.

Down the hall were two small bedrooms. Each had a full-sized bed and dresser. Only one room had a small TV.

"You can have the room with the TV," Mom said walking past me.

That meant she wouldn't be home much.

The kitchen was fully stocked. The best part was there were two bathrooms. I didn't have to share it with anyone.

"Are there washers and dryers here?" Mom asked the landlord.

"Yes, there is a coin laundry room downstairs," the landlord said.

"This is nice, mom. What do you think?" I asked.

"We'll take it," she said.

"Great let's go fill out the paperwork," he said.

Mom and I moved in that same day.

At seven a.m., the sun rose in Breckenridge peeking over the mountain. At the same time my alarm clock buzzed for several seconds. I kicked my sheets off and retreated into my small bathroom. The hot water cascaded over my body and washed the night off me. I blow-dried my hair and got ready for my first day of school.

"They better not have a dress code here," I shouted stepping into the kitchen.

"And if they do?" Mom yelled back.

I stood in front of the open refrigerator. I scanned the cold empty shelves and then slammed the refrigerator door. "And how will I get to school if you have the car all day?"

"You'll have to walk," she said. "Remember, we chose this apartment because it was close to school."

"Can't you buy me a car?" I asked.

"With what money?"

"I don't know. Can't you call grandma?"

"If you want something, call your dad." I mouthed along with her.

I shoved my jacket in my backpack. "I'm leaving."

"Not so fast, missy. I'm driving you to school today."

"Why? You said I had to walk, remember?"

Mom put on her only pair of shoes. "Don't get smart with me. I have to register you for school and pay to enroll you."

"With what money? And I thought this was a public school."

"It is a public school, but you still have to pay for somethings. And don't you worry about how I'll get the money. I'll think of something."

I'm sure you'll think of something, and that's what I'm afraid of. Maybe you should ask Dad for it.

"Fine, I'm ready. Let's go." I stomped to the door.

"You're wearing *that*?" she asked.

"I'm wearing a tee shirt and jeans. It's school, not prom. And you don't need to come with me. I can register myself."

"I want them to know you have a mother," she said, following me down the second story staircase.

"Really? When will she be here?" I mumbled. Dragging my backpack, I dashed to the car.

We pulled into the almost-full parking lot at the high school. "Summit High School, Home of the Tigers" was painted on the front window. Open football and soccer fields butted up to the evergreens. White aspens swayed in the wind with Breckenridge Mountain nestled in the background. I couldn't believe I would be going to a school with such amazing scenery. We had nothing like this back in Illinois.

An enormous mural was painted in the foyer—a crouching orange and black tiger ready to pounce on its prey. "Tiger Pride" scrawled above it in a huge script. This was the school's mascot. Our mascot back home was a Royal—a man dressed in a long blue velvet robe. A gold crown sat on his crooked, oversized head. My Royal days were over.

We entered the principal's office where a view of the mountains could be seen through the floor to ceiling windows behind the desk. An announcement blasting through the loudspeakers reminded students there was still time to register for the fall hike.

"Hi, I'm here to register my daughter for school. We moved here from Chicago a few days ago," Mom told the secretary standing behind the counter.

I offered my best fake smile.

"Oh, how nice. Welcome to Summit School," the secretary said, smiling. "Why don't you have a seat, and I'll let Principal Adams know you're here."

Mom sat down first on one of the five wood chairs outside the principal's office. I sat two seats away from her and set my backpack on the floor.

Students entered the school wearing faded unripped jeans, athletic and collared shirts, and sweaters, both button crew and V-necks. Most of their clothes were white and various shades of green, their school colors. I sighed in relief. I was just like them. We were the same. They were no better than me. It was 8:10.

Come on, Mrs. Adams, what's taking so long? Ugh.

Finally, the principal emerged from her office. "Come on in and let's get you registered," she said warmly.

We entered her office. A collection of photos of her and of the school's students and athletes, as well as athletic awards and diplomas from different universities decorated her walls.

"I'm Sarah Adams, the school principal." Her lips turned into a smile when she extended a hand to Mom. "Please sit."

"Good morning, this is my daughter, Sandy Kelly, and I'm Mary Somers." Yep, her name was different than mine—there was a husband number two, but he didn't last too long either. I don't even remember the guy. His name was the only thing that stuck around.

"Hi," I said to Mrs. Adams. I sat in the chair closest to the door in case I needed a quick escape.

"Welcome to Summit High School, Sandy. Do you have your transcript from your last school?"

The answer was no, my mother did not get my transcripts. She only thought about herself and getting out of town before the mafia found her. Not really, but because mom still hadn't told me why she had to leave, I was going with that, it was more interesting.

"Don't worry. We'll get them," Mrs. Adams picked up the phone. "Berta, we have a new senior starting today. Her name is Sandy Kelly. Can you please call Austin High School in Chicago and have them send over her transcript? And you'll need to prepare a class schedule for her. After we get her transcript, we can change her schedule if we need to." She hung up the phone. "I'm sure you're ready to start your day, so let's fill out the rest of the paperwork and get you to your first class."

Mrs. Adams handed some forms to my mom to fill out. "Sandy, do you have any hobbies?"

To be honest, my hobbies were hanging out with my friends and partying, but I was sure she didn't want to hear this.

"Uhm, I like sports. I took tennis lessons once," Was all I could come up with.

After a few minutes, Mom handed the completed paperwork to Mrs. Adams. The door opened.

"Hi, I'm Berta, you must be Sandy Kelly."

"Yes, I am."

"Here's your schedule," she said, handing it to me. She rested her hand on my shoulder and made eye contact with me. "Karen Bartlett will be your counselor. She will call you down to go over your schedule and make sure you have everything you need. But if you need anything before then, please don't hesitate to see me. I'm always here in the office."

I glanced at my schedule, seven hours of school. Back home, my last class was over at 2:20 pm. I got out early because I had a job at the bank after school. Like Mom said, if I wanted anything, I had to get it myself, so I did. I earned my own money. When I was eleven, I had a paper route, and at fifteen, I worked at a clothing store that my mom's boyfriend owned.

"Thank you," I said, smiling at Berta.

"It looks like everything is complete," Mrs. Adams said. "Ms. Somers, here is the breakdown of the fees for the year."

My mom shifted in her chair. "Money is tight right now. Is there another way to work this out?"

I slumped in my chair. Oh my god, what was my mom trying to do?

Mrs. Adams sat back and swiveled in her chair. A smile crossed her lips. The chair stopped. She rested her hands on her desk.

"Well, we're starting a girl's tennis team this spring, and we're looking for players." She volleyed her gaze between us. Her eyes fell on me. "I can waive the registration fees and the tennis fees if Sandy is willing to join the tennis team."

"Of course. She'd be happy to play tennis," Mom said.

I glared at my mother.

What? Are you kidding me?

You're selling me to the tennis team for what…two hundred dollars?

Shouldn't I have a say in this?

Thank God I didn't tell her I was a cheerleader and a gymnast. I had quit both. Most of my friends were not into sports. I was the jock in the group. I was the one who had bruised ribs, hips, legs, and arms. My friends nicknamed me "Strapper." This was my last year of high school. I wanted to enjoy myself, and I didn't want to compete with anyone anymore or commit my time to anything. I wanted to do what I wanted to do. I didn't want my body broken anymore. But here I was joining the tennis team.

Mrs. Adams was waiting for *my* answer.

I sat back in my chair and shrugged half-heartedly. "Uh, yeah… Sure, I'd love to play tennis."

Go Tigers!

I glanced at my mom. She smirked—She hated me.

Mrs. Adams's door opened and a girl dressed in designer clothes entered her office.

"Clarissa, this is Sandy Kelly. She just moved here from Chicago. Please show her around today and tomorrow if needed," Mrs. Adams said.

Clarissa and I stood shoulder to shoulder, but she was curvier than I was. She wasn't a size two, but then neither was I. Regardless, I doubted we could have worn each other's clothes, and her boobs filled out her shirt way more than mine did. Her blonde hair sparkled in the sunlight shining through the windows. I'm sure she gets a lot of attention from the boys. The makeup she wore was heavy, like she was covering more than her skin. I wondered what she was trying to hide.

I jumped out of my chair and flashed a fake smile at Clarissa. I had to leave this office before my mother committed me to the track team too.

"Hey," Clarissa and I said in unison. I grabbed my backpack, swung it over my shoulder and headed out the door. I didn't say goodbye to my Mom. She could stay there all day if she wanted.

THREE

Capricorns enjoy puzzles and difficult games

Monday, 8:30 a.m.

Clarissa and I wove around students in the crowded school halls. Several guys we passed paused and turned their heads with lifted eyebrows. Some of the girls glared. They weren't checking me out like the guys were. Before we got to my first class, Clarissa showed me where the library and bathrooms were.

"So, The Windy City, huh?" Clarissa asked.

Ugh, why does everyone say this mentioning Chicago?

"Yep, The Windy City."

"How long have you been in Breckenridge?"

"We got here two days ago."

"I hope you don't think I'm nosy, but do you have a boyfriend back home? I'm sure everyone will be asking," Clarissa said.

"No, I don't have a boyfriend. And even if I did, it wouldn't matter anyway."

My last boyfriend broke up with me. His old girlfriend, who moved to Arizona in August and wasn't supposed to be back until June, convinced her parents to let her come back early and live with her older sister after she found I was with her ex. Either way, that bitch stole my boyfriend. But, of course, I moved on.

The bell rang as we got to my first class. The teacher was sitting on the edge of his desk, hands in his pockets. Clarissa handed my paperwork to him. "I'll see you after class," she said, leaving.

The classroom was the same as any other history class. Posted on the walls were dates of hard-fought wars and pictures of famous generals and presidents.

"Welcome to first-period history. I'm Mr. Carlson. Everyone, this is Sandy Kelly; she just moved here from Chicago."

Every pair of eyes in the class was on me— all 25 of them.

Ugh, stop staring already.

Mr. Carlson reached into a desk drawer. "Here's a history book for you, Sandy, and there's an empty desk over by the window next to JD."

I slid into my chair and glanced out the window at the ski slopes that rose above the evergreen treetops. The barren runs crisscrossed the mountain disappearing in the trees. Wow, what a nice view. But had a better view next to me. I couldn't help but look at JD. Well-developed muscles strained against his shirt sleeve when he raised his arm to run his hand through his hair, and long legs stretched under the desk in front of him. He must have been a baller. I was thinking football or basketball. This was what I would have pictured a Greek God to look like. His thick coffee-brown hair was pulled back and held in place with gel, and dark eyebrows framed his chocolate brown eyes, which were staring into mine.

I think he's seducing me with his eyes.

Is this normal for first period class? I think I'll play along.

I lowered my shoulder and cocked my head in his direction. His left eyebrow inched upward, and his lips curved into a smile.

"Take out your notebooks and write down the class assignment," Mr. Carlson said.

Out of the corner of my eye, I caught JD checking me out. I shifted in my chair. My heart fluttered when our eyes met. I didn't have a game plan yet. I needed more time to analyze this situation. I tried to avoid eye contact.

He leaned toward me. "I'm JD McCarron. Do you have a pen I can borrow?"

I thought it was odd he'd been in this class for at least a month, and didn't have a pen. I unzipped my backpack and pulled out my favorite blue pen. I offered it to him but pulled it back before he could take it. I had to let him know I was in control. I straightened my shoulders. "Oh, and this is my favorite pen, so if I don't get it back, I'll come looking for it," I said.

JD winked. "Promise?"

Oh, my god.

Heat rushed my cheeks and throughout my body.

It was hard to pay attention to the teacher talking about the Boston Tea Party with JD sitting next to me. And who cared about the tea from Boston anyway? I think I missed something because I was too busy watching every move JD made with my pen. I mean, it only made sense that I had to keep my pen in sight, right?

Forty minutes later, the bell rang—history was over, and Clarissa was waiting for me at the door. After we left class, I tried to see which direction JD had gone without being too obvious, but I lost him in the crowd.

"So, Clarissa, do you have a boyfriend?" I asked.

"Yeah, his name is Jason. We've been going out since seventh grade." A smile spread across her lips. "He can make you laugh and want to pull your hair out all at the same time. This is a small school, so I'm sure you'll meet him soon."

I was glad she didn't say JD was her boyfriend. I wonder how she was able to stay with the same guy for five years. Didn't she get bored? Did she ever feel smothered by him and the relationship? Five years was a long time.

After we turned the corner, she pointed. "There he is, over by the water fountain."

She was pointing, but my attention was on JD, who was standing there with the other guys. His demeanor was so confident. "Which one is Jason?"

"He's the tall blond with the navy-blue shirt. And next to him is JD McCarron. The greatest quarterback in Summit history. So he thinks," she said.

"Yeah, I kinda met JD. He's in my history class."

"I'm sure you'll see him with a group of girls hoovering and acting stupid."

We turned down another hallway and headed to my next class.

* * *

1:04 p.m.

Sixth-hour P.E. I checked in with the teacher. She handed me a pair of dark green shorts, a white t-shirt, and a padlock and pointed toward the girls' locker room.

"Go change and when you're done report back to the gym," she said.

After I changed, I checked myself in the mirror. My new gym clothes matched the color of my eyes. I rolled my shoulders back and nodded in approval. I ran my fingers through my hair, pulled it into a ponytail and hurried back to the gym.

I joined the rest of the class, and the teacher started taking attendance. JD chatted with a group of guys near the basketball hoop.

I wonder if he's done with my pen.

"When I call your names, I will announce what team you will be on and then we'll head out to the soccer field," the teacher yelled out.

I was not on JD's team; I was his opponent. JD better watch out on the field. When I was younger, I loved playing sports and competing with the boys. I wanted to prove that even though I was a girl, I could still kick their butts at anything we played, even in a skirt. Losing was not an option for me. But, as I grew older, boys got bigger and stronger too. I had to find a different way to prove I was just as good as they were. I had to get in their heads.

Out on the soccer field the teacher handed out blue shirts to JD's team. JD pulled his shirt over his head and glanced in my direction from across the field. I was going to let him chase me first, but I had to remember that anyone who was a baller *and* that good-looking was probably a player, too. Hopefully, JD wouldn't be like *him.* He was an athlete, too, but his game was dominance. I won't let anyone control me—to hurt me like *he* did again.

I needed to be careful.

I locked my eyes on JD and tried to hold his attention. I pulled my hair out of my ponytail and slowly brushed it off my shoulders. JD's eyes followed my movements as I tilted my head.

Maybe I'm a player too.

The teacher blew the whistle and rolled the ball out onto the field. I tied my hair back and joined my team on the field.

JD's team controlled the ball first, passing it ball back and forth, traveling down the field. I stayed back and kept my eyes on JD while my teammates tried to block and steal the ball. I pulled my ponytail tighter. Neither the soccer ball nor JD were going to get past me. I positioned myself, ready to attack and defend.

One of JD's teammates kicked the ball downfield. JD and I both ran toward the ball, which stopped about ten feet between us.

JD's teammates yelled, "Kill it, JD, Kill it."

Our eyes locked on each other like lions hunting their prey. Neither of us blinked. We both ran full speed toward the ball. We were only a few feet away from each other—he had the edge on me. I couldn't get to the ball before JD. I had no choice but to slow down to avoid crashing into him. JD pulled his right leg back and then swung it forward, connecting with the ball in a powerful kick. It flew at me. There was no time for me to get out of the way. I turned my body and covered my head. A second later, the ball smacked into my butt. I dropped to my knees. My butt was on fire.

"Oh, shit," JD said as he bent down to help me up. "Are you alright?"

I slowly rose to my feet, brushing the grass and dirt from my knees. "Yeah, I'll live."

"Ah, I thought you would back down, but you didn't," JD said.

"Nope, I never back down," I said.

I don't know what hurt the most— my butt or my humiliation of letting JD get to the ball first.

"Oh, my team is about to score," he said as the ball flew through the net. "Yes!" he cheered.

"Congrats," I said.

JD just smiled.

Back at the sideline, I watched JD celebrate with his team. In the distance, a whistle blew three times.

"Great game, everyone. Make your way back to the gym," the teacher said.

The game was over *or, was it?*

I headed toward the locker room, and JD ran up to me.

"So, uh, how do you like Summit School so far?" he asked, running his hand through his hair.

Yes, your hair still looks good.

"Uhm, it's good so far, other than getting hit in the butt with a soccer ball." I laughed.

"Sorry about that."

"It's okay. I'm still trying to find my way around, *and* I'm missing my favorite blue pen."

"Don't worry, I still have your pen," he laughed, pushing my shoulder. "Where do you live in Breck?"

"Breck?"

"Breck is short for Breckenridge. I can see I need to teach you a few things around here."

"Ah, yeah, I live right down the street from school, and I'm sure you'd love to teach me some things," I teased.

JD blushed. "Well, I'd be happy to show you around. What kind of things do you like to do?"

We stopped outside the girls' locker room. "Well, I—"

The bell rang, cutting me off.

"We'll talk later," JD said and shuffled backward toward the boys' locker room.

Four

Capricorns don't dream of fancy worlds

On my way home, I talked to a few other students who were headed in the same direction I was. A black Jeep Wrangler pulled over onto the shoulder of the road, gravel crunching beneath the tires.

"You never answered my question," JD yelled out the window.

I stepped toward his Jeep. "Saved by the bell, I guess."

"Ah, good one. Want a ride home?"

"I'm good," I said, looking into the passenger-side window. "I'm only a few blocks away."

I continued walking on the side of the road. He followed in his Jeep, glancing at the road and then back at me.

"It's on my way. It's no problem."

He stopped.

"JD, do you want to give me a ride home?"

He nodded, and a giant grin crossed his face. "Yes, I'd like that."

I climbed in.

He pulled on to the road. A mocking smile flashed on his face. "I'm glad I got to you before anyone else did."

"Oh, yeah, right. I'm sure there was a line down the block waiting to drive me home."

A deep laugh escaped his throat. "So, other than soccer, what else are you good at?"

Oh my god, I loved his laugh. It was so real. "Ha, very funny, and I'm good at everything." I caressed my hair as I tipped my head in his direction.

"Wow." His eyes widen. "Do you seduce every guy like this?"

He was so much like me. "No, only guys who drive black Jeep Wranglers." I focused back on the road. "This is my driveway here. You can let me out at the staircase."

"So, since you're new in town, do you want to hang out this Saturday? I can show you around, if you're not too busy, of course." He winked.

A guy with a great sense of humor. I liked that. "Tell me what you have in mind, and I'll let you know if I'm busy or not."

He chuckled. "Ah, you're killing me here. Well, we, I mean, my friends and I hang out at the rec center on the weekends. Have you been to the rec center yet?"

"No. Where is it?"

"It's right outside town. The rec center has everything. They have indoor tennis courts, a track, a fitness center, and an indoor pool. You name it, girl, we can do it."

"Okay, but what about horseback riding? I saw a ranch outside of town that has horses."

JD grimaced. "You're probably talking about the Carrillo Ranch. I'm game to do anything but horseback riding. Plus, I don't like the guy who lives there."

"Who is that?"

"Never mind."

"All right. Let's go to the rec center. Do you run?" I asked.

"Yeah. You want to go for a run in the morning?"

"Yes, and then you can show me the rest of the rec center after. I mean, if you're not too busy." I winked at him.

"All right, sounds like a plan." Before I got out, he rested his hand on my thigh.

I lifted his hand, placed it on the seat, and climbed out of the jeep. "Thanks for the ride. Oh, and do you seduce every girl like this?"

JD cleared his throat. "I'll pick you up at ten." A blush moved across his face before he pulled away.

Yeah, he's a player, or maybe just a flirt.

* * *

A few days later the phone in our apartment was finally hooked up, and I could start calling my friends back home. I sat on my bed, head propped up on the headboard, and called my best friend Holly. Holly and I met a couple of years ago at gymnastics camp at Southern Illinois University. We borrowed each other's clothes and hung out at her house, where we practiced our balance beam routines in her backyard. We did everything together. We were like sisters, except we never fought or argued. We watched out for each other. It was strange we had never met even though we only lived five blocks away from each other.

"Oh, my god, Holly, I'm so glad you answered."

"Hey, gurl, how are you doing? And why didn't you tell me you were leaving?"

"I didn't know until the last minute. I was trying to find a way to stay but…I…"

"Don't worry about it. At least you called."

"I'm okay, though. I didn't even ask you how you are doing."

"I'm good. But I miss my bestie."

"I know. Me too."

"Everyone's been asking what happened to you."

"Tell them aliens kidnapped me, or the mafia got us," I said.

"I will. They both sound interesting. Speaking of aliens, how's your mother?"

"I don't know. Still the same. I think she met a guy already. I haven't seen much of her since we moved here."

"What? It's only been a couple of days?" Holly asked.

"Yep. Maybe it's someone she works with. Or whatever. Anyway, she never says anything other than don't wait up, and there's money on the table for dinner."

"Sounds like things haven't changed much."

"Nope, only the scenery. It's so beautiful out here. Holly, the ski resort is so awesome."

"How's your new apartment?"

"Ah, it's alright. At least I have my own room and phone. I have a great view of one of the runs from my living room. I wish I knew how to ski."

"You'll learn someday. Did you take your chalkboard?" she asked, laughing.

"No, I left it. Sometimes I think about it, but it's yours if you want it."

"Nah, I'm good. It wouldn't be the same without being able to watch you cross guys' names off it."

I laughed. "Yeah, I know. So, who's having all the parties since I've been gone?"

"A few people. The parties aren't as good as yours though."

"I didn't think I was going to like it out here, but I met the hottest guy at school this week," I said.

"Nice, tell me about this hottie."

"Well, first of all, he's a jock." I stared up at the ceiling and pictured JD in my head.

She laughed. "You never dated a jock here."

"I know. Maybe I should have." I giggled. "We're going for a run at the rec center on Saturday."

"Oh my god, you are such a dork. Who goes for a run on a date?"

"Me, I guess. He's a total flirt, and he's throwing everything he's got at me."

"And I'm sure you're making him work for it, too," Holly said.

"Of course I am." I caught my reflection in the mirror. "I haven't changed. I really miss everyone back home."

There was silence on both ends of the phone.

"Hey, Holly I have to go. I have to get dinner ready before my mom gets home."

"What's for dinner?"

"I went to the store after school and bought stuff to make Goulash."

"That sounds good. Call me later and let me know how your boring running date with the hottie goes," Holly said.

"Haha, funny. Bye, Bestie."

* * *

Friday after P.E., JD approached as I was walking to my seventh hour class. "Hey, Sandy, are you coming to the game tonight?"

I nudged his arm with my shoulder. "Oh, is there a game tonight?"

He pointed to his green and white number twelve football jersey with a grin. "That's why I have this on. There's also pep rally seventh hour."

"Yeah, I can make it unless there's a line of guys waiting to ask me out."

"Haha." JD made a show of looking behind me for the line of guys. Or was he looking for someone else?

"Oh, are you playing?" I teased.

His eyes narrowed. He straightened his back and smiled. "Don't you know I'm the best quarterback since the beginning of time?"

I laughed inside. "I don't recall anyone saying the beginning of time."

"Good luck tonight, JD," a couple of girls yelled out as they passed us in the hallway.

"Groupies?" I asked.

JD ran his hand through his hair. "No, I don't have groupies," he said.

Maybe he wasn't a player after all. "I guess I'll be there," I said.

JD scanned the hallway again. "Good. I hope I'll be able to concentrate on the game instead of you tonight."

Uhm. I might have been wrong. Maybe he was a player after all. "Well, if you don't concentrate on the game, I'm sure there will be a linebacker ready to take you out," I said.

"Funny girl. It will never happen. My guys protect me at all costs. So, meet me outside the locker room after the game. Then we'll go out for pizza and head out to some parties."

"Ahh, parties, now you're speaking my language."

"I'll see you later," he said.

When I got to the game that night, I saw Clarissa. She waived me over.

"Come sit with us," she said.

I squeezed past some students and sat down.

"Sandy, this is Tammy."

Tammy and I both said "Hi."

"The game is about to start," Clarissa said.

Drums beating and horns blowing from the band playing the schools fight song filled the night air, hyping the mood. Cheerleaders yelled "Let's go, let's fight, let's win tonight! Goooo Tigers." as they formed two lines on the side of the home tunnel. They stretched a white paper banner with an open-mouthed green tiger hungry for another victory across the tunnel's opening. The Tiger mascot ran up and down the Tiger sideline coaxing the fans to cheer. The smell of freshly popped popcorn lingered in the air, making my stomach growl.

Everyone was on their feet, clapping, pumping their arms, and yelling "Tigers, Tigers!"

An announcement came from overhead. "Ladies and Gentleman, I'm Pat Jacobs, and I'll be announcing the game tonight with my good friend Ron Adams. Welcome to Summit High School, home of the Fighting Tigers. Tonight, Summit High School is hosting the Keystone Cougars who are 3-1. Please put your hands together and cheer on your Tigers. Here they are."

The players charged through the banner, shredding it.

Out on the field, JD shouted, "Who are we?"

"Tigers!" The team shouted back.

"What are we going to do!?" JD yelled.

"Defend this house!" They yelled back.

Both teams took their positions for the kickoff. JD was standing on the sideline. He turned toward the stands. He saw me and pointed. I nodded back. A few girls who were sitting in front of me turned to see who #12 was pointing at.

"Clarissa, what number is Jason?" I asked.

"Jason is #34, and Jamison, Tammy's boyfriend, is #42," She said.

The Cougars kicked off to the Tigers. After the kick the Tigers took possession on the 36-yard line.

"Sandy Kelly, I'm Dan, the tennis coach." He squeezed in between Clarissa and I. "Principal Adams told me you were joining the team."

"Ah, yeah. I guess I am," I said.

Clarissa and Tammy laughed.

"I'm really excited about you joining the team. How about meeting at the rec center and getting some practice swings in before the season starts?"

"Sure."

"Let's meet tomorrow morning," Dan said.

"I can't. I have plans tomorrow morning."

"Sunday morning then, say, ten?"

"Yeah, I'll be there. But I don't have a racket," I said.

"I'll bring a racket for you. See you Sunday."

After Dan left, Clarissa and Tammy teased "Jock."

Thirty-five minutes later, in the fourth quarter, the crowd was restless. Parents were shouting at the coaches, throwing out plays. The cheerleaders weren't cheering, and the mascot was hopping around holding its oversized Tiger head.

"This is a tight game." Clarissa said.

"We can't lose, we can't lose," Tammy added.

"Folks, it's starting to get chilly. The Breckenridge Tigers are trailing the Keystone Cougars 27-24. The undefeated Tigers are 4-0 and only have just under two minutes left in this game. Starting at the 36-yard line with 64 to go. Just one score will take the lead. With one timeout remaining, it looks like Coach Herb Bradley is gathering his offense to put together this one final drive. And now we are inside the two-minute warning here in the fourth quarter. The Tigers trail by three. Field goal to tie and touchdown for the lead as the Cougars try to break the streak on the road. With one timeout and 1:58 on the clock, it is all down to #12, JD McCarron, and the rest of the Tigers."

The tigers huddled and then broke. They lined up on the 36-yard line.

JD was a few yards back behind the center. On the right side of him was his running back Jason Edwards, three receivers on the right, and one on the left side. The play clock was running down.

"Down! Set, Hut! Hut!" The ball was snapped on a two count. JD caught the snap at his chest. He ran toward Jamison Thompson, his running back for a fake handoff. Jason ran up the middle between the center and right guard but was stopped. JD looked to his right and found Jamison on the outside line. He passed it, a little wide but Jamison caught it and stepped out of bounds.

"Thank goodness #42, Jamison Thompson, ran out of bounds to stop the clock. Still about 60 yards to go until the score," Pat said.

"Watch the clock," Coach Bradley yelled, pointing at the clock.

The referees put the ball down as the Tigers huddled up.

"So, Ron, what do you think JD McCarron is saying to his boys right now?"

"He should be telling them We need a win to stay undefeated."

"Here we go, folks," Pat said.

"Break!" The Tigers clapped their hands and lined up.

JD assembled a few yards behind the center with Jason on his left. Two receivers were on both sides of the offensive line. "Down. Set. Hut!" Jason caught the snap and ran towards the right side.

"It's a running back direct snap play, Ron." Pat announced.

Jason spun halfway around to underhand it a few yards back to JD. JD put his hand on the laces. He found Jamison open. JD hurled the ball, it was caught by Jamison. He tucked it under his arm and ran up field but was tackled in bounds by a Cougar's safety.

"That play, folks, was a flea flicker thrown to #42, Jamison Thompson. Brought down by #43 on the Cougars. First down from around the 50-yard line."

"On the line! On the line!" JD ordered.

"The Tigers are going with a no huddle."

"Down. Set. Hut!" JD yelled. The snap was a little low but JD held on. He looked right quickly and then left. He threw the pass over to #11, who caught it over his shoulder. Inches away from running out of bounds, he was brought down short by #22 on the defense.

"A gain of about nine. Giving us second and short with clock running around a minute and a half," Pat said.

"The Tigers offensive line is doing a good job of protecting their quarterback," Ron added.

"On the line! On the line!" JD ordered.

"Another no huddle for the Tigers. The clock is ticking away," Pat said.

JD quickly scanned his lined-up teammates. He scurried over to Jason and tapped the right side of his helmet. "Down. Set. Hut!" JD took the snap and handed it off to Jason. Jason tucked the ball and ran to the right. He was brought down.

"A gain of three. A first down on the Cougar's 38-yard mark. The clock is now at 1.3 seconds." Pat announced.

"On the line!" Ordered JD. The Tigers raced back to the line. JD took his position behind the center. "Hut!" He took the snap and spiked it in the ground.

The clock stopped.

"A spike brings us to second down and ten with the clock stopped with 1 minute left. The Tigers are still holding onto one timeout."

JD jogged over to Coach Bradley and Coach Myer. They tapped JD on the helmet.

"I wish we could hear what Coach Bradley and Coach Myer are saying," Ron said.

A few seconds later, JD jogged back to his huddle. The Tigers were ready.

"Break!"

Jason and his receivers squeezed together as if they were building a wall. "Ready," Jason yelled flapping his arms upwards and nodded at Jamison. All the receivers moved out toward the line.

JD scanned the line. "Down. Set. Hut!" The ball was snapped. He took two steps back. He looked for Jamison, who was ten yards down running straight towards the sideline.

"JD is holding back. He's lining it up for Jamison, #42 to catch the ball. Hopefully he'll be able to run it out of bounds to stop the clock." Ron said.

JD connected with Jamison. He cradled the ball in both hands. As soon as he got a foot down, he was tackled by #31 from the defense.

"It's under a minute left and a first down on the 27-yard line. JD is acting as calm as a cucumber," Pat announced.

The Tigers were on the line. Jason was lined up as a left tight end. Two wide receivers were on both sides.

"McCarron is taking his time," Ron said.

"Down! Hard 90! Hard 90! Set! Hut!"

The two wide receivers dropped back two yards. Jason raced upfield. JD threw the ball up and long. Jason pivoted inward keeping his eye on the ball. The ball landed perfectly in his hands. He ran a few yards and into the endzone. The referees whistle blew.

"Touchdown. It's 30-27 Tigers with 27 seconds left of the game!" Pat Shouted.

"Coach Bradley is holding up two fingers at JD. The Tigers are going for the two-point conversion," Ron added.

JD signaled for a huddle.

"I wish I could be a fly on the wall in that huddle." Pat said.

"Break!"

JD was outside left in wide receiver position as Jason lined up on the opposite side.

"This is very interesting. #42 Jamison Thompson is going to have the ball snapped to him," Pat said.

Jamison yelled. "Down. Blue 64. Set. Hut!" The ball was snapped. He ran up the middle but there was an opening. He rushed right. #55 of the Cougars was on his tail. Jamison turned. He tossed the ball to #19 on the Tigers. #19 spun around but was brought down quickly, inches away from scoring.

JD and his offense slumped back to the bench, heads down.

The Tigers special team kicked off to the Cougars. The kicker launched it straight about 30 yards before it bounced.

#44 on the Cougars picked up the ball and ran. The kicking team was there to greet him. #44 took a knee.

The clock stopped with 17 seconds left of the game.

The ball was on the Cougars 42-yard line. The Cougars lined up. The ball was snapped.

"#17 drops back for the Hail Mary. Everybody is deep. He airs it long. Ohhh and overthrown," Pat announced.

The Keystone Cougars lined up again. "Down. Set. Hut!"

"It's a low snap. He's running with it. #17 is charging forward. And he is forced out of bounds by the Tiger defense. A gain of nine. This will be the last play of the game, Folks. This is the game right here."

The fans were on their feet. The night air was bursting with the banging of metal from the fans stomping their feet in the stands.

The Cougars lined up.

"Down. Set. Hut!" The Cougars Quarterback #17 took the snap.

"He's got time. The Cougars line is holding. Their receivers are now waiting for the ball down field. This is it. #17 launches the ball. How is this going to end, folks?" Pat shouted.

Everyone turned as the ball flew into the darkness downfield. As the ball started to descend there were a total of ten players from both teams waiting in the end zone.

#26 of the Tigers jumped up to grab it but all he could do was swipe it down. #13 of the Cougars dove toward it but the ball hit the ground. The horn blew.

"TIGERS WIN! TIGERS, WIN!"

Clarissa, Tammy, and I hi-fived each other.

After the game, I stood outside the locker room with everyone else waiting for the other players to come out. The bright lights on the building formed circles on the cement below. When JD came outside, his hair was still wet, and he was dressed in regular clothes, no jock football uniform. I watched him for a few seconds then stepped into the light. When our eyes met, he lifted his head and walked towards me. Several people approached JD with pats on the back and handshakes.

"Great game, JD."

"We knew you would pull off the win," a couple of men said.

"Thanks, man." JD answered.

JD walked over to me. "Thanks for waiting." He tugged his casually fitted jeans up. I got a nice view of his tight abs when he raised his arms to pull a dark blue sweatshirt over his head.

Yep, this was worth waiting for.

"Great game, it was a real nail biter," I said, moving my eyes from his body to his face.

"Yeah. Thanks, 5-0 so far. I'm starved, are you ready to eat?"

"Where are we going?"

"Ridge Street Pizza on Ridge Street. Have you been there?"

"No, not yet."

"Good. You're in for a treat," he said.

"Nobody does pizza like Chicago. I think it will be hard to beat a Chicago deep-dish pizza. Have you ever had one?"

"Nope. I can't say that I have."

"Well, it's baked in a deep-dish cake pan, like an upside-down pizza. You pretty much have to eat it with a fork. The Mozzarella cheese is on the bottom, on top of a crunchy-edged buttery cornmeal crust. Oh, it's so yummy. And then a chunky tomato sauce is piled on top."

"I like any kind of pizza, except if there are mushrooms or pineapple on it. Who the hell puts pineapple on a pizza?"

"I like pineapple on my pizza, but not in a deep dish."

"You are crazy," JD chuckled.

"Ha ha, maybe I am crazy. I'm not a fan of the New York-style pizza. New Yorkers call it a slice. The crust is soft and they cut the slices really big and you have to fold it to eat it."

You either loved deep-dish or you didn't. In Chicago, there was a rivalry with the style of pizza you liked and with a Chicago baseball team. If you lived on the North side, you were a Cubs fan. If you were a Southsider you were a Sox fan. You couldn't be both. If you liked both you'd never admit it. I was a die-hard Cubs fan, but I liked the White Sox too, I loved anything Chicago.

"Who else is coming?" I asked.

"A few players and friends. Clarissa and Jason, Tammy and Jamison will be there."

"How long have you and Jason been friends?"

"Since grade school. Our dads are both lawyers, they work together. Clarissa's dad's a doctor. See the house up on the hill with all the lights on? She lives up there. So, you're covered if you ever need a doctor or a lawyer."

"Good to know." What was I getting myself into? I wondered if JD had ever gone out with a girl like me. He seemed normal, and I hoped he didn't have a "my father's a lawyer" wardrobe. I was graphic tee and jeans girl. Back home, I never liked the guys who came from money. They acted like they were the important ones instead of their parents. Plus, they were boring—good-looking but boring. So far JD wasn't boring. He was actually a nice guy.

"And what about you? Which house is yours?" I asked.

"You're full of questions tonight, aren't you?"

"I'm only trying to find out who all the players are," I said.

"Well, I don't live up on the hill. Let's leave it at that."

I wondered why he said that.

Was he afraid I'd judge him based on where he lived?

Did girls or even guys treat him differently because he was the star quarterback? Did others only want to hang out with him because he was cool and they wanted to be cool, too? Back home, a few girls wanted to hang out with me because I had parties all the time and I had a lot of guy friends. They wanted to be part of all that. I didn't mind so much. I knew they were using me. Because the more girls got to know me, the less rumors were spread about me being a slut and whore.

After we ate and the armchair quarterbacks recapped the game, we left. We parked a block away and walked down the car-lined street to the house. JD brushed his hand against mine until our fingers found each other's.

At the house, JD handed a ten-dollar bill to a very giddy party goer and grabbed two red Solo cups. He took my hand again, and we zigzagged around athletes and experienced partiers, while we made our way to the keg in the backyard. The song *Takin' Care of Business* rocked the house, along with high pitched laughter from drunk girls. Couples were kissing and caressing each other in the hallways and in every room.

The parties I hosted at my house were like this one, except there were no jocks or cheerleaders. They didn't hang out with me, or should I say I didn't hang out with them. I didn't see any candles burning or smell any incense either. I was pretty sure if there were any lit candles, they would be burning the house down with all the chaos. My parties were a lot classier than this one.

JD pumped the keg a few times between high-fives with friends as they called out "Great game, JD." He grinned while he filled my cup and handed it to me, then filled his own. He swallowed his first beer and refilled his cup.

"Drink up," he said, tapping his cup to mine.

I raised my cup and let the golden liquid slide down my throat as quickly as I could. We stood outside for a few minutes, taking in the night air. We stepped back inside. The base from the music vibrated in every room. We tried to find a quiet corner, but we still had to lean in so we could hear each other. JD pressed his body into mine. His breath tickled my neck when he talked. A shiver raced down my spine when I inhaled the scent of his sandalwood soap. This was nice.

While we talked, I got a few glares, and it was obvious people were whispering about us or maybe just me. They cocked their heads and flashed fake smiles at me. Ah, screw 'em. I drank my beer and focused all my attention on JD—he was the reason I was here, and he was the one I was going home with. Well, the one who would be driving me home.

"Do you want another beer?" JD asked.

"Are you trying to get me drunk?"

"I don't know, will it get me anywhere?"

"No…it won't," I said.

"So, one's your limit?" JD asked.

"For now, it is. I don't get drunk or smoke pot when I go out with guys I don't know very well."

JD wrinkled his forehead, and his eyes searched mine waiting to hear more, but then he looked at his watch and sighed.

"Time to go?" I asked.

"Yeah, I have to be home by one."

"Just like Cinderella?"

JD gave a brief laugh. "Very funny. No, my parents are so lame sometimes. What's your curfew?"

"When the seven dwarfs come to get me." We both laughed. "I don't have one." I took both our cups and set them on the table next to us. "But, I'm ready to go."

"So, why no curfew?" JD asked.

"I've never had one." I took a minute to try and remember when the last time I had to be home was. "Except when I was young, if I wanted to eat, I had to be home by 5:30."

"So, let's go back to when you said you don't drink around guys you don't know very well," JD said on the way back to his Jeep.

"I had a nice time tonight. Did you?" I asked, avoiding his question.

"Ah, yeah. I did, too."

"The pizza was good. The party was nice, and the beer was cold. But you could have scored a few more touchdowns tonight, JDog."

He laughed. "JDog? Nice… And it makes sense. I can see how JD is way too long."

We stopped at his Jeep. His lips took possession of mine. When our lips parted, I pulled him back into me and kissed him again. I hadn't kissed a guy for several months. I liked it.

I liked JD. But something seemed off. People at the party gawked way too long at us talking.

"Great game, JD! Way to stop them damn Cougars!" Yelled a couple of guys walking towards the house.

JD waived. "So, I was wondering…"

"I'm cold, I think we should go," I said.

"Ah, all right," JD said.

We got in his Jeep and he drove to my house. When we got there, he pulled up to the staircase.

"Are you ready for tomorrow?" he asked.

"Yeah, I can't wait to see if you can keep up with me."

"You're on, girl." He smirked and winked. His hand brushed my hair off my shoulder. "Can I steal another kiss for the road?"

"Nope, you'll have to wait until tomorrow," I said, shifting away from him.

"Ugh…" He groaned, looking up at the roof of his car. "Fine, I'll see you at 10 am sharp. And don't keep me waiting, sleeping beauty," He said.

I held a smile on my face all the way to my room.

FIVE

Capricorns are ambitious, relentless, and persistent

The next morning, JD picked me up at ten o'clock on the dot.
"Are you ready to get beat at your own game?" JD asked, as I jumped in his Jeep.

"Yep, I'm ready, JDog."

"I hope you brought a water bottle."

I held my stainless-steel bottle up. "I have my water bottle right here."

"Good because you are going to need it," he joked.

"We'll see," I joked back.

We pulled into the parking lot. The rec center was nestled in the foothills of the ski slopes. Rising beyond, yellow-leafed birch and pine trees snuggled at the bottom of the mountain.

JD checked in and registered me as his guest.

"This place is so awesome," I said.

"Yeah, it is. You'll love working out here…with me."

A guy walking in behind us called out. "McCarron! What's up?"

"Hey…, Carrillo." JD took my hand. "Let's go upstairs, Sandy."

"Who is that?" I asked.

"Ah, nobody."

I wondered what was up between those two?

The running track upstairs overlooked the gym and reception area. I stretched my hamstrings, took a big drink of water, and set my bottle on the bench next to JD's.

"Ready?"

"Ready!"

We started out with a slow jog. The view of the mountains out the floor-to-ceiling windows was a great backdrop for running. I imagined I was running outside along a trail hidden on the mountainside. The people we passed on the track were the forest animals on the trail. The music playing overhead inside was the rustling of leaves on the ground and the whistling of the tree branches in the wind. We didn't have any place like this back home. I had to either run in the street or at the track at the high school.

"So, why jogging on our first date?" JD asked.

"Oh, is this a date?"

"Ah, what do you want to call it?"

"I wouldn't call it a first date. And I guess jogging helps clear my head when I'm frustrated." My lungs felt void of air. I took a deep breath in.

"What would you be frustrated about?"

"I don't want to talk about that now."

"Okay. We'll talk about it later. I don't run other than at football and basketball practice, and then I'm not clearing my head. I'm only running for endurance and to keep the coaches off my back."

We passed a few slow joggers. I noticed they were breathing okay.

"And what is with all this Country music playing everywhere?"

"It's because this is Colorado. You're in the West now." He grinned. "What kind of music do you listen to?"

"Anything but country." I tried to fill my lungs again, taking short breaths. My mouth started to get dry.

"Get used to it, because we listen to a lot of country music here."

"Yeah, I know. It's hard to find a radio station that isn't playing it. I mean, come on, how many times can you sing about an empty whiskey bottle, a broken guitar string, and a dog who's run away?" I barely got all that out in one breath. What was going on?

A giant grin spread across his face. "You know country music pretty well." He laughed.

"I wish I didn't. I guess I'll have to introduce you to some good 'ole rock and roll."

We finished our first lap, and I stopped beside the bench where our water bottles were. I clutched my stomach and held on to the bench. "I-can't breathe. I think- I'm going-to pass out."

JD pulled me out of the way of the other runners. "I don't think you're used to the altitude yet."

"No, I'm not—but that's the only reason—I'm stopping. Not because—I—I can't keep up."

"It takes a while to get used to the air up here. Try breathing through your nose, not your mouth. And if that doesn't help, I'll give you mouth-to-mouth."

I rolled my eyes but I couldn't help but laugh. "Thanks. I'll let you know if I need it."

JD helped me over to the bench. I sat and rested my cheek against the cool window, taking a drink of water.

"Catch your breath yet?" He squirted water into his mouth.

"Yeah, it's getting better. It's my—turn to ask questions now." I said.

"Take another drink of water first," JD insisted.

"I'm okay. So, JDog, do you have a girlfriend? I hear rumors at school that you do."

JD lowered his head. "I hate rumors, and well, yes and no."

Damn, why was he chasing me if he had a girlfriend? I knew he was a total player. I could spot a player from a mile away.

"And?"

"Jessica and I have been going out for two years."

This news wasn't helping me breathe any better. I stared at the floor. My hopes dashed away. Oh well.

"We don't even talk anymore. All we do is fight, a lot. She complains about everything I do. She's ridiculous. And all she talks about is cheerleading."

I should have known better to get involved with him. "Uhm, yeah, I was a cheerleader, but I quit."

"Why?"

"I didn't fit the cheerleader profile. I hated the practices and the constant primping, and I hated having to behave myself all the time."

"I suspected you were trouble."

"Whatever. And don't change the subject. Where *is* Jessica today?"

"She's at some stupid cheerleading camp. She and a couple of other cheerleaders left last night after the game." He tossed his bottle back and forth between his hands.

I took a deep breath and stood. I didn't know what to say. I was disappointed he had a girlfriend, but then here he was with me. "I'm better now. You want to finish our run?" I asked.

JD tugged me back down. "No, not yet… I'm not done with my questions. Do you have a boyfriend?"

"Here?"

"No, back home, or anywhere?"

What did he want? What should I do? I'd play it cool. I should tell him I have a boyfriend back home and see how he likes it. "No. I don't have a boyfriend," I said. Maybe I'd show him what he was missing out on.

"Good." He dropped his bottle, and it rolled under the bench.

"What? Why is that good? Are you…"

"So, why did you come to Breckenridge?" He reached under the bench and grabbed his bottle.

I followed his movements. "I don't know, I guess it was time to leave."

"I'm glad you're here, because I have a weakness for girls with green eyes. Wait, your eyes *are* green, aren't they?" JD winked.

"Thanks for changing the subject. And yes, they're green. Don't you think you're laying it on a little thick?"

JD laughed. "You can't blame a guy for trying, can you?"

"Yes, I can. You are such a flirt."

"So are you," he said.

JD's observation caught me off guard. Maybe I did flirt too much. How else did you get people to pay attention to you?

I didn't dress slutty like some of the girls in school. So, I flirted. I wanted people to notice me, to like me. If you liked a guy, weren't you suppose to show it? Back home, everyone knew me. They either liked me or they didn't. I didn't care either way because I didn't have to pretend to be anyone but myself. Many times, I wondered if my friends really liked me or if they only liked me because my mom let them party at my house.

"The worst part about being here is I miss my friends."

JD scooted closer to me on the bench. We faced each other.

"You'll make new friends. Everyone in Breckenridge is nice. Besides, you already have one friend."

I jokingly pushed his head away.

"I could talk to you for hours."

"Really? My grandmother told me I talk too much."

"Well, I don't see your grandmother here, so keep talking. Tell me more about yourself," he said.

"No, I'm done talking about me."

"All right, Uhm, well, ah…"

"Are you having trouble breathing? Do you need some water?" I offered my water bottle to him.

"Do you want to…"

I stood and backed away from the bench. "Let's finish our run. And bring your water. It sounds like you might need it," I said.

While we ran a few more laps, all I could think about was telling an almost perfect stranger things that made me feel a little vulnerable. He saw a weakness. He called me out for flirting, but he didn't laugh when I told him what my grandmother said. I needed someone to tell me they wanted to hear my voice. Unlike my mother. When I was young, my mother would grab me and sternly whisper in my ear, "Children are to be seen and not heard." A chill ran through my body.

When we finished our run, JD drove me home. He pulled up to the staircase.

"Isn't Jessica going to be mad you're with me today?" I asked.

"I don't really care if she gets mad. I'm breaking up with her."

"Why?"

"Because I want to go out with you," he said.

"Uhm…"

"So, ah, do you want to go out with me?"

I wanted to say, "yes," but Jessica had to go before JD got me. *Jessica has got to go*, Jessica has got to go. "I don't go out with other girl's guys."

His mouth dropped open. I guess he was used to getting what he wanted. Kind of like I'm used to doing what I want.

"So, no, not now," I said confidently. If he wanted me, he was going to have to prove he wanted only me.

He jerked his head back. "Wow. Okay. I thought last night you were into me. I mean, that kiss…"

I held back a smile. "I am, but..."

"So…"

"You have a girlfriend, JD." Please don't be the player I think you are. Please prove me wrong. I don't want every athlete to be *him*.

"Not for long. I'm going to end it," he said.

A smile tugged at my lips. "So, end it, and then I'll go out with you. But not right away."

"Then, when?" He asked.

"Give it two weeks. I don't want people to talk," I said.

He spread his hands. "Talk about what?" He asked.

"About me breaking you and Jessica up."

His body tensed and then relaxed. "I don't care what people think, and neither should you."

"It's different for girls, JD. Guys aren't called whores and sluts."

"Hum, I wouldn't mind being called a whore." He smirked.

"Not funny, JD."

He rubbed his hand over his face and nodded. "I know. I guess I have some work to do tomorrow."

"Until then, we'll hang out as friends," I said.

"Fine. What are you doing tomorrow?"

"I have to meet Coach Dan at the rec center for some tennis practice."

"All right. What are you doing next Friday night after the football game?"

I shrugged.

"Good, I'll pick you up, and we'll hang out."

"As friends," I added.

In response, JD pulled my head toward his. He nudged his nose against my chin, lifting it, and our lips found each other's. This kiss was way different than the one we shared last night. His tongue parted my lips to sweep over my tongue, teeth and then back over my lips. He was a pretty good kisser. I should know, since I won the kissing contest when I was thirteen, and then again when I was fourteen. His minty toothpaste lingered in my mouth when he pulled away. I wasn't sure when the last time I kissed a friend like this was, but I liked it. He was doing a good job workin' it, or, I should say, workin' me.

I pulled away. "This doesn't solve your Jessica problem."

He shrugged. "No, but it solved my kissing problem."

* * *

Saturday morning, I met Dan on the tennis courts.

"Good morning, sunshine," Dan said.

"Hey."

"I'm glad you were able to make it today. Have you played tennis before?"

"I took lessons, and played on a team the summer before I started High School."

"Well, let's see what you got." Dan bounced a few balls in my direction.

"Coach Dan, how's it going?"

I looked over. It was the same guy I saw yesterday.

Dan patted him on the back. "Tom Carrillo. It's been awhile. What's new with you?"

"I was getting a few matches in with my brother. Other than that, just work." He waived in my direction. "You have a new student?"

"Yep. This is Sandy Kelly. We are getting some practice in before the season starts."

"I'll let you get back to your lesson. It was nice to see you Dan and nice to meet you Sandy, Take care."

Uhm, don't go, you can stay here as long as you want.

"Yeah, see you later. Hey, Tom, come out and watch our matches when you have time."

"I'll definitely do that, Coach."

"So, where were we?" Dan asked.

My eyes were glued to Tom as he left the tennis courts. 'What?"

Dan shook his head. "Earth to Sandy…Let's get back to our lesson."

For the next hour, we hit the ball back and forth, working on my forehand. Dan showed me how to grip the handle and how to slide my hand around in a circular configuration. It was nice having Dan work with me today. I wish I had someone back home or anywhere that took an interest in me. Working with him made me want to be better. I think I'm going to like being on the tennis team after all.

"Can you come practice after school a few days a week?" Dan asked.

"Yeah, I guess."

"You're very apprehensive. Do you not want to play tennis?"

"My mom made a deal with Principal Adams that I would play tennis because she didn't have any money to register me for school."

"Ah."

"But I'll play. I don't have anything else to do."

"Good. I'm glad you're here. I think with some practice and my expertise instruction, I can make you a star."

I laughed. "Did you play tennis in High School?"

"I sure did, in High School and in College."

"Where did you go to College?"

"University of Central Florida in Orlando."

"Was it very expensive?"

"Yes, very expensive. More than my parents could afford. But I got a partial scholarship and I worked part time at Disney World to pay for the rest."

"Did you have to dress up as a mouse or something?"

"Ha. No, I was not a mouse. I did various jobs, like stocked shelves in the stores, sweep the grounds. Stuff like that."

"Were you any good?"

"At cleaning and stocking?"

"No, at tennis."

"Okay, now we're back to tennis." A smile lit up his face. "Yeah, I was pretty good. Are we done talking about me now?"

"Yeah, I suppose. I'm just making sure I have the best tennis coach coaching me."

"Trust me you have the best coach. Let's call it a day. We'll work on your serve and backhand next week. How did you like the racket?"

I held it up and inspected it, running my hand over the strings. "I think there might be something wrong with it."

Dan's eyebrows arched. "How so?" He took the racket out of my hand and ran his fingers over the strings.

"Well, for one, it missed a few balls, and then, when it did connect, the ball hit the net. A couple of times."

Dan shook his head, smiling. "Ah, I see. I'll make sure you get a different racket so you won't have any more excuses."

"Sounds good, Coach Dan. I'll see you next week," I said, walking backwards towards the door.

"Oh, by the way…He's too old for you," Dan shouted across the tennis courts.

Friday night, JD picked me up after his away football game. Jason and Clarissa were in the back seat.

"JD, where are we headed?" Jason asked.

"To the park to hang out for a while." JD pulled onto the road and drove toward the park.

"What's Jamison and Tammy doing tonight?" Jason asked.

"They're meeting us there," JD said.

"Can we have a bonfire, or is it still fire season?" Clarissa asked.

"We're good," JD answered.

"What is fire season? I asked.

"Fire season is when there is a high risk of fires because of the heat and wind. So they won't let you burn anything outside. It's usually over in late September," JD said.

JD pulled off the road. His Jeep rocked back and forth, driving over gravel on the uneven shoulder. He peered into the rearview mirror. "Jamison and Tammy are pulling up now."

I got out of the Jeep, and the cool evening air hit my skin. I pulled my jacket tighter around myself.

"You cold?" JD asked.

I shoved my hands deeper into my pockets. "A little."

JD wrapped his arm around me. My body softened against his touch. We stepped through a clearing in the trees to an open area where others had previously set up a makeshift fire pit. The guys hauled fallen branches and logs from the brush and tossed them into the firepit. The sweet scent of pine hit my nose. It reminded me of the candles I burned at Christmas back home.

"The fire's ready," Jason yelled. The smoke billowed into the air while the flames crackled against the cool night air.

JD patted Jason on the back. "Nice work, Jason. Sandy, grab a seat, or should I say, grab a tree stump."

"Sandy, come sit by us," Clarissa said. She slid over on one of the fallen trees.

I sat beside her and pulled my hands out of my pockets to warm them over the fire. To my left, Jason, Jamison, and Clarissa were talking about what they were doing tomorrow. On my right, Tammy was leaning toward JD.

"Where's Jessica? I saw her at school yesterday. She didn't seem too happy," Tammy asked.

I held my breath waiting for his reaction.

"We broke up. I'm surprised Jessica didn't tell you," JD said.

"No, she didn't say anything." Tammy looked over at me. "Oh. So, you're going…"

"Ready for a little truth or dare, folks?" Jason asked.

Perfect timing Jason. Even though Truth or Dare is a stupid game where only guys win.

"Really, Jason, truth or dare? Aren't we a little old for this?" I asked.

"Hey, Chicago, don't get crazy now. You don't mind if I call you Chicago, do you?"

Was this guy for real?

"Whatever makes you happy, Jason," I said.

"Good. So, to answer your question, no, we're never too old, and besides, how else am I, or should I say we, going to get to know you?"

"You could just ask and not make me play this stupid game."

"Nope, we're doing it my way. Now, sit back and relax." Jason slid his hand up into the bear-proof lid of the trash can, pulling the lid down from inside. Bears didn't know how to reach up and engage the inside latch. This was designed to keep bears out, but not Jason. He pulled out an empty Coke bottle and shook the brown residue out. "I'll go first." He scraped his boot along the ground, clearing the pebbles and pine needles before setting the bottle in the dirt and spinning it. "Stand back, here it goes."

He circled his hands above the bottle as it spun. The bottle slowed and stopped on me.

"Nice." A wicked grin flashed across his face as he stroked his imaginary beard like a villain plotting his move. "Alright, Chicago, truth or dare?"

I took a deep breath and pursed my lips.

"Come on, Chicago. Truth or dare?"

"God, Jason, I'm thinking. Gimme a minute." I rubbed my hands back and forth on my jeans.

"Time's up, Chicago," Jason said.

I was getting a feeling Jason was going to be my Villain for the rest of this game and maybe even after. "Okay. Jason, truth."

"What?" Jason asked. "Truth? Damn. I was hoping you would say dare."

"Well, I'm saying truth."

"Damn, girl. Let me think about this." Jason paced back and forth, kicking up dirt.

I started to dread my answer. "Can I change to dare?" I asked.

"No. It's too late."

JD, Clarissa, Jamison, and Tammy leaned forward.

"Damn. How should I ask this? Alright, I'm ready. Are you still a virgin?"

A collective "Ooh" came from the group.

JD pointed at me. "You don't have to answer that."

"Shush, JD," Jason said.

I wondered if Jason knew JD wanted to go out with me, and Jason didn't want him to. I couldn't let him know this bothered me. "It's okay. I've got no shame in my game," I said.

JD rolled his eyes toward Jason. Clarissa's knees were bouncing. Tammy and Jamison sat motionless.

"Nice. Then spill it, girl," Jason said.

"Geez, Jason, do we really need to know this?" Jamison asked.

"Yes, and I'll tell you why later." Jason scowled.

I swallowed hard. My eyes met JD's. "Yes," I said quietly.

"What? What do you mean, 'yes'?" Jason asked.

"Jason, don't you remember your own question?" Clarissa asked.

"Shush, C. My question, Chicago, is, are you a virgin?"

"I told you my answer is yes."

Jason's eyes flashed with shock. Everyone's jaws dropped.

"Wait, girl, didn't you have any boyfriends back in Chicago?"

"Yes, Jason, I had boyfriends, but that doesn't mean I slept with them. And if you were so sure I wasn't a virgin, then why did you ask?"

Jason sat next to JD. "I don't know. But the bigger question is, why didn't you sleep with them?"

I was so embarrassed but I wasn't going to back down. I searched everyone's faces. They lowered their heads. I hoped at least one of them would jump in and help me out. Maybe they were afraid Jason would ask them the same question or worse. I guess I was taking one for the team. I surrendered.

"I guess I didn't want the responsibility." It was a stupid answer. I didn't have a better one. Maybe it was one of my Capricorn traits that held me back. Like the one where I wasn't a risk-taker, or not impulsive, or maybe I didn't want to get pregnant or get any nasty STDs. But the real reason for not having sex was I didn't know how. I liked the way my life was— the fairy tale stayed alive if I didn't have sex.

But deeper down inside, I wasn't ready to have another guy control me and my body.

Jason threw his arms up. "What responsibility? All you have to do is drop trou and go for it."

I raised my eyebrows in amusement. They all laughed. I hesitated before I laughed along with them. I couldn't believe Jason just said that. I hoped he would finally drop it.

"I don't want sex to be about dropping trou and going for it," I said.

"Girl, really?" Jason continued. "No sex? Didn't you want it?"

Oh my god, you are such an asshole, Jason.

"You're not gonna let this go, are you?" I asked.

He shook his head. "What are you waiting for?"

I should have just crossed my legs and stopped talking.

"Are you done now, Jason? You got your answer, and you made your point," JD said.

Jason picked up the bottle and handed it to me. "Your turn, Chicago."

I squatted down off the tree stump and set the bottle on the ground. I twisted the bottle and let it go. I stepped back and waited for it to stop. It landed on Jason.

"Nice." I tapped my finger on my chin. "Payback time."

"Fire away, Chicago. Ha, get it? Chicago Fire?"

"Yeah, I get it," I said.

"Let's go then," He rubbed his hands together. "I'm ready for you."

"Give me a minute to think."

I've got to get him back.

"Dare him to do something stupid," Jamison goaded.

"Ask him about the time he—"

"Shut it, JD, and Jamison," Jason said.

Jason pointed at Clarissa and Tammy. "And she doesn't need any help from either of you guys. Tick-tock, Chicago."

"Shut up, Jason," Clarissa scolded.

"Chill, C," he scolded back.

"Okay, Jason, truth or dare?" I asked.

His lips tightened. "Truth," he said.

"If you weren't dating Clarissa, who would you want to go out with?" I smirked.

JD, Jamison, and Tammy slid back on their logs, covering smiles. Clarissa glared at Jason.

"And it doesn't have to be a female either if that's your thing," I added.

"Ooh! Ouch," echoed through the forest.

JD high-fived Jamison.

"Yeah, yeah, funny, Chicago," Jason replied.

"Answer the question, Jason, who?" Clarissa demanded.

Jason wiped the sweat from his forehead. "I hate you, Chicago. I'm going to play it safe and say Mrs. Thomas, the librarian."

Everyone giggled. Clarissa shook her head. And even though it was dark outside, the glow of the fire illuminated Jason's red face.

"No wonder you spend so much time in the library, Jason. I'm never going to let you live this down," Clarissa teased.

"Thanks, Chicago," Jason snapped.

I kinda like this game now.

"No prob." I took my seat, leaving the bottle in the dirt.

"My spin again." Jason picked the bottle up, brushed it off and spun it with such force the bottle skidded in the dirt.

Everyone watched the bottle like it was life or death. Sighs of relief filled the air when it landed on JD.

"Yes!" Jason rubbed his hands and blew into them. "I gotta make this a good one. JD, brother from another mother. Truth or dare?"

JD shook his head and took a deep breath. "Dare."

"Nice, JD. This is going to be fun," Jamison snorted.

Jason folded his arms. "JD, you know I could dare you to do a lot of things right now, but I'll go easy on you."

"Bring it, Jason," JD said.

"Okay, okay. I dare you to say something to someone here. Something you've wanted to say for a long time," Jason said.

JD cocked his head. "Alright, you're a dick, Jason." JD winked at me.

I smiled back.

Thanks, JD.

"JD, man, why would you say something like that to me? Besides, I'm the bottle spinner."

"I like how you make the rules up as you go," Clarissa jumped in.

"Yeah, quit being a dick, Jason," Jamison said.

"JD has the floor, not you," Jason corrected Jamison.

We sat in silence and waited for JD's response.

"Sandy, I don't want to wait two weeks."

I sighed in relief. I didn't want to wait either.

Everyone looked around at each other.

"Wait, what?" Jason interrupted. "What's that supposed to mean?"

JD and I smiled.

"I'm game," I said.

JD stood and extended his hand to me. We headed to his car.

"Wait, where are you two going?" Jason asked.

"Game over, bro. I've got a date," JD answered.

Six

Capricorns are rock solid, can control urges

The next day, I called Holly. "Hey, Bestie, what's new back home?"

"Nothing much. Same old, same old. How was your date with the hottie?"

"Good. We're kinda going out now," I said.

"Nice."

I sprawled across my bed and looked out my window at the treetops. "I told you he was chattin' me up and laying it on pretty thick when we first met, right?"

"Yeah…"

"I found out he had a girlfriend," I said.

"What? What a jerk!"

"I told him I wouldn't go out with him until he broke up with her, and he did."

"Good to hear. What's his name?" Holly asked.

"JD, but I call him JDog. Don't ask me why. I have no idea where I get these nicknames."

"Have you made any other friends yet?" Holly asked.

"Yeah, mostly JD's friends. We played Truth or Dare last night. Can you believe it?"

"What? Are you kidding me?" She asked.

"No, and one of JD's friends actually asked me if I was a virgin."

"Oh, god. Did you lie or tell the truth?"

"I told the truth," I said.

"Right in front of JD?"

"Yep, he'd find out anyway if we kept going out."

"How brave of you. Do you think JD's the one?" Holly asked.

"You mean to finally lose my V card to?"

I don't know. Could JD be the one?

Wouldn't a bell ring, letting me know this is the right guy?

"Maybe. I've got to make sure he's not playin' me," I said.

"Oh, girl, relax. Guys are always playin us, and us girls are always playin' them. Get really drunk or high and just go for it, for God's sake."

I sat up.

Did I really need to get drunk or high to have some guy take me?

What if I drank too much and threw up all over him?

How much fun would that be?

"I need to make him wait a little more, though. I guess I'm not as brave as you are. You still there?"

"I'm not that brave either," Holly said.

I flopped on my bed.

I guess I never thought about if she was or wasn't a virgin.

Part of me wished she wasn't so she could walk me through it.

But I was glad I wasn't alone either.

"Really?"

"Never mind. Oh, and there's one more thing I need to tell you."

I shot up onto my knees. "What?"

Holly was quiet for a second.

"What, Holly?" I asked again.

She hesitated and then quickly said. "Rusty and I are going out."

And then silence.

"Really?" I asked when the silence dragged too long.

"Are you okay with this?" Holly sheepishly asked.

I don't know— am I okay with this?

Think, think, think.

"Yeah, why wouldn't I be?"

"Well, you two did go out for a long time."

"But that was two years ago, and we were on and off. Rusty is a good guy," I said.

"Yeah, I know, but I don't want this to ruin our friendship," Holly said.

"Don't worry about it. We will always be friends. Who else would I exchange clothes with?"

"You're not here though. I'll stop going out with him if you want me too."

Can she read my mind all the way from Chicago?

"No. I don't want you to do that. Are we okay, Holly?"

"Yeah, we are okay, we will always be okay. Hey, Rusty just rolled up. I gotta go."

"Tell Rusty I said hi."

"I will. Oh, and don't call me until you've lost your V card. I want to hear all about it."

"No pressure there, right?" I forced a laugh.

"Ciao, sweetie," She said.

"See ya." I slowly lowered the receiver and hung up. I curled up into a ball.

Oh my god, I feel like I don't belong anywhere.

My mom is still never home.

Jason treated me like a pariah, and Holly is moving on without me— with my old boyfriend.

I'll be okay, I have to be okay.

* * *

I found a note in my locker after school on Friday. Before I read it, I checked the hallway. It was empty. Classroom doors were closed.

JD McCarron requests your presence at his
18th birthday party.
When: Saturday, October 15, at 3:00 p.m.
Where: The rec center. Meet in the pool area.

"Are you going to come?" JD stood beside me. He wore his practice football gear and held his helmet.

"Ah, you scared me." I closed my locker. "Yeah, of course I'll come, and how did you get this in my locker?" I waived the note in front of his face.

"I have my ways. I'm glad you can come, but I can't pick you up. I have to go early and help my parents set up so..."

"I'll have my mom drop me off."

If I can convince her to stay home for a few hours.

"How many people are coming?"

"Everyone," he said.

"The whole school?" I asked.

"No. Not the whole school. You'll know everyone, so, don't worry. And don't forget to bring your swimsuit. I gotta go. I have to get to football practice, I'll call you tonight."

Mom wasn't happy she had to stay home Saturday until three o'clock to take me to JD's party. She wanted me to walk like I did everywhere, every day. I lied to her. I told her I hurt my foot during P.E. the day before and it hurt to walk on it. I wasn't sure if she believed me or not, but she did give me a ride.

She pulled next to the curb. I hopped out of the car. "Thanks for the ride."

She yelled. "It looks like your foot is feeling better now." And drove off.

Ugh. Why did she always have to call me out?

JD was right. Everyone was here. Some were in the pool, and others were hanging out by JD while he was setting up the table with pop and snacks. Over in the corner was a table with wrapped gifts.

"I'm glad you made it. Go change and I'll meet you back out here," JD said.

I changed into my black crochet bikini and met him back at the pool. His forearms were black and blue, probably from football. His powerful arms were folded against his chest.

JD's eyes lit up when he saw me. "Now I have something to dream about tonight."

I hope that's all you wanted for your birthday because I didn't have any money to buy you anything.

Heat spread across my cheeks. "I'm glad I could help." I held my hand over my stomach. "I forgot my towel. Do you have an extra one?"

"Yeah, we have more towels. I'll grab one for you later," JD said.

JD's parents walked over to where we were standing. JD's dad was an older version of JD. Same dark hair and dark eyes. His mom was blonde with blue eyes.

"JD, would you like to introduce us?" his mother asked.

"Um, yeah, this is Sandy Kelly. She moved here a few weeks ago from Chicago," JD said.

I shook their hands. Mrs. McCarron's eyes traveled down to my stomach.

"Is that a ring in your belly button?" she asked.

I covered the blue sapphire hanging from my belly button with my hand. "Yes, it's a piercing," I said.

"Wow. Did it hurt?" She asked.

"Yes, it did." I could use that towel now, JD.

"Let's go for a swim, Sandy." JD took me by the hand and led me to the deep end of the pool. We jumped in and swam to the side.

"I don't think I scored too many points with your parents, did I?"

"It doesn't matter. You did with me, and that's all that counts." JD pointed at the top of my right breast. "How did you get that scar?"

I rubbed my hand over my scar, feeling where the stitches were. "I had a benign tumor last year and had to have surgery to remove it."

"Benign…?"

"It means not Cancerous. It's all good. I just have an ugly scar now."

"Did it hurt?"

"No, not—"

A volleyball came crashing into the water between JD and me, splashing both of us.

"Jason, you're dead," JD yelled out.

"Quit talking and let's play some volleyball, JD," Jason yelled.

"Yeah, let's kick his ass, Sandy," JD said.

We played a few games of volleyball. JD and I kicked Jason and Clarissa's butt's both times, but that wasn't the best part. The best part was when I jumped to hit the ball, JD pulled me down into the water and wrapped his hands around my waist. When I opened my eyes, his face was a few inches from mine. Air bubbles float out of his nose, making me laugh. I had to surface quickly before I swallowed a pool of water.

At the end of the day, everyone's skin was as wrinkled as a 100-year-old man. After swimming, we changed back into our clothes and ate pizza, and then went into the movie room. The room was small—it probably held about 50 people. Popcorn and pop were on a table in the hall outside the movie room.

"What movie's playing tonight?" I asked JD.

"Grease."

How ironic, a story about a virgin named Sandy who moved to a new town, met a boy, and fell in love.

"I know this movie pretty well," I said.

"Good, but don't tell me how it ends," JD said.

"I won't."

JD and I sat next to each other. He rested his arm over my shoulder. During the movie, he whispered in my ear. A shiver ran down my spine. I pulled away from him.

"Are you alright?" He asked.

"Yeah, your breath tickled my ear. That's all." Maybe it was romantic to have a boy whisper in your ear. But I didn't like it—I hated it when anyone did this—especially my mother.

"I was going to tell you I wish we were alone right now."

"Me, too," I said.

He kissed me. When our lips parted slightly, he turned to see if his parents were watching. The coast was clear.

The following Saturday night, JD and I drove to an ice-skating arena outside of town next to the outdoor The Highline Railroad Museum. Before we went skating, JD showed me several locomotives that ran in the late 1800's. A huge black rotary snowplow was used to clear the snow off the tracks allowing trains to bring supplies into town during the winter months. The front of the snowplow had a large round jet turbine fan attached to it. As it plowed down the track, the center blades opened and spun, cutting through the snow and ice that had formed on the tracks. This snowplow was so heavy that it took six locomotives to push it while it threw snow 30 feet on each side.

At the indoor -outdoor ice-skating arena, JD and I skated around the perimeter of the outdoor rink until I got the hang of it. I hadn't been on ice skates in years. The cool night air kissed my face as I glided on the ice. The sharp cold frozen smell hit my nostrils. Little girls dressed in pink tutus spun in circles, carving up the ice and twirling like graceful swans. The sound of their skates scraping along the ice made me jealous at how they moved so easily.

Every time I wobbled, JD was there to keep me from falling. "Don't look down. You'll fall forward. Keep your head straight for balance," JD said.

Once I got my balance, we skated into the middle of the rink to attempt some Olympic jumps.

"JD, can you do a triple sow cow?"

"What the hell is a triple sow cow?"

"It's a jump skaters do." I raised my arms and twirled around. My left skate hit my right blade. I wobbled until I fell to my knees.

"Just like that, huh?" JD asked.

"Well, not actually."

"Come over here by me, so you don't fall again."

We skated for another hour and then rested on the bench, drinking hot chocolate.

"I'm done. My legs are so killing me," I said.

"You need to work those legs more. I can help with that if you want."

"Nope. I don't need your help. I'm not that kind of girl."

JD laughed. "I think I heard that somewhere."

"Very funny. I don't think Jason likes me. He came down on me pretty hard the other night."

"Yeah, Jason can be like that sometimes. He likes you. He's got two older brothers who are away at college. And he tries to be like them but ends up being something he's not."

I knew exactly what JD was talking about. Sometimes, I wanted to be someone else, too. I didn't want to live in the shadow of my mom's reputation. I wanted to be myself, but I didn't know who that person was. Every time I tried standing on my own two feet, my mother knocked me down. I built walls around myself when people wanted to hurt me. I built a fort that nobody could enter.

"You were pretty cool about the game. Thanks for being in my corner," I said.

"It was just a game."

We finished our hot chocolate and left. About a mile west from town, off a side road, JD found a quiet place and parked at a lookout point. The overlook showed the whole u-shaped valley lit up below.

"Do you know how Breckenridge got its name?" JD asked.

"No, how?"

"The town of Breckenridge was named after an old prospector - Spencer Breckinridge, which was spelled with an I after Breck. But then he pissed some people off, and the town changed the I in his name to an E. so it was enridge instead of inridge. What a total dis."

"Thanks for the history lesson," I said.

He puffed out his chest. "I told you I could teach you a few things."

JD scanned the radio stations for anything that wasn't sports commentary or country music. "Will this do?" He asked.

"Oh yeah, I like Bob Dylan."

"What's your favorite song of his?"

"I love 'Like a Rolling Stone,' but I like a lot of his other songs too. The stories he tells in his music are interesting."

JD unbuckled my seat belt and pulled me to him. We kissed for a while, and then he unzipped my jacket. His hands explored my body over my shirt. I shrugged out of my jacket and pulled my shirt over my head. A smile overtook his face. JD reached around to unhook my bra. His hands pressed against my back, over and over, but my bra remained firmly in place.

"Undo." JD murmured into my shoulder.

"Do you want help, or should I let you struggle?"

"Help, please," he said quickly.

I unhooked my bra. The straps fell off my shoulders, exposing my breasts. He took them in his hands and lowered his face into my chest.

His mouth found my skin as his hands pressed into my sides. I cringed at the discomfort as his mouth circled my boobs like prey.

Why can't guys take their time? They aren't going anywhere, and no, they both won't fit in your mouth at the same time.

I felt his tongue on my nipples and then a sharp pain.

"Ow, that hurt."

"Sorry," he whispered. He smiled, and then pressed his wet lips hard against mine.

"Let's get in the back seat," he said boldly.

We jumped out of the Jeep, quickly climbed into the back seat, and kicked our shoes off. He laid me down and started to remove my jeans. My skin tingled as his hands explored my body. His fingers circled around my belly button and then down between my legs.

Yes, keep going.

He unzipped his jeans and pulled me toward him. He took my hand and positioned it between his thighs.

Oh, God.

He pushed me back down and moved on top of me. I was ready to let JD take me.

I had dreamed of this touch, his touch, of this very moment.

But was now the right time? Shouldn't I be staying in control? I didn't hear any bells ringing either. I need to be in control right now.

It was so difficult, the way he caressed my breasts and nibbled at my throat. A warm sensation surged through my body. It felt so good, but I needed to be strong. He lowered himself onto me. His weight was unexpected, and his hands grabbed at my thighs.

"I want you so bad." His breath was hot against my ear. He held me tight.

I couldn't turn away. His words repeated in my head. My heart raced. I wanted this, but I couldn't breathe. I closed my eyes and tried to erase the helplessness I felt the last time someone held me down. I didn't want *him*—I was only ten. This was different. I wanted JD. I took a deep breath. My chest rose to meet his. I wondered if I pushed him away and told him I didn't know how to do this if he would break up with me?

I hated the way I felt. I couldn't do this.

I've said 'No' so many times before because saying no was the only control I had in my life. Except for *him*, he didn't take no for an answer. I wasn't giving it up that easily. I couldn't let anyone take control of me again.

I raised my hands between us and pushed against his chest. "JD, I'm not ready for this," I said.

"Oh, *you* are very ready," he said.

"I mean…"

"Don't you want me?" He asked.

"Please, stop."

He backed off. "Why, what's wrong?" His voice was strained.

"Uhm, I gotta ask you, JD—are you playing me?"

He tilted his head while I retrieved my shirt from the floor and wrapped it around myself.

"What? Playing you? Why would you ask me that?"

I needed to come up with something other than I wasn't ready. "There's a rumor going around school that there's a bet to see who can get me into bed first," I lied.

He sat up, not taking his eyes off me. "Who did you hear that from?"

"Girls around school," I said.

"They're saying that because they don't want you going out with their boyfriends. And I can only assume Jessica was one of them."

"Maybe."

"You know you're the first girl who's ever told me to stop? And, no, I'm not playing you at all…I'm not that guy. The first time I saw you in history class, I wanted to talk to you. But I was too scared to say anything except to ask if you had a pen I could borrow. How stupid was that? And then I wanted to ask you out when I gave you a ride home, but I chickened out again. So, if I were playing you, I would have tried to get you into bed a long time ago." He held my face in his hands. "I like you, and I want you to trust me. I've noticed every time I come close to you, you pull away…"

I sat up next to him. "I'm fine. Uhm, I don't like people whispering in my ear," I said.

"Okay. Is there anything I can do…?"

"I'm okay. I like you too, JDog. I have a great time with you, and you make me feel good when we're together. But I need to make sure you're not playin' me or using me for--"

"I need you to trust me on this… Please?" JD said.

I didn't like having to lie about the rumor going around school, but I needed to hear JD tell me how he felt about me. I wanted to know he liked *me*.

"I want you to wait until I'm ready. And I need to know I can trust you."

He leaned back on the seat and stared at the ceiling. I needed to think fast. I really liked him and I didn't want to blow my chance with him completely.

He went to zip his pants up, but I put my hand on his. "No, wait, not yet. I'm not ready for that, but it doesn't mean I'm not willing to do other things." I took a deep breath. My heart pounded. I needed to do a decent job of this. I slid down between his legs and looked up at him. A smile covered his face. I needed to finish what I started. Occasionally he thrust his hips forward and held the back of my head, pushing himself down further than I would have liked.

Am I supposed to enjoy this, too? Or just him?

His groan gave me the validation I needed. He finished sooner than I expected, but pulled away before he released.

I satisfied him. I guess this is what I'm supposed to enjoy.

I sat back up beside him holding my wet hand out front. "Ah…"

JD handed me a towel from behind the back seat. back.

"Thanks." I wiped my hands and the seat off. "Please be patient with me?"

"I'm good," he said breathlessly. He put his arms around me and laid me down on the seat. I rested my hand on his chest and felt his heart pounding. "Your turn," he said confidently.

His fingers trailed down my stomach and circled my inner thighs again. He maneuvered his way down my body and buried his head between my legs. I placed my hands on top of his head to help him out, but he seemed to know what to do on his own. He was good, and he didn't mess around. I wanted to enjoy what was happening, but lying to him still bothered me.

God forgive me for lying.

And then, I finished. My mind relaxed, then my body.

He still wanted me.

Seven

Capricorns are fluent in sarcasm

My Mother liked Scotch. The scotch bottle was the first thing she picked up when she got home from work. A while ago, she showed me how much to pour into the glass and how much water to add. She told me several times it would be nice if I had one ready for her when she got home. I didn't agree.

I didn't like scotch. It smelled like a sharpie marker and had an earthy taste, like wood. I also didn't like it because it was what made my mother happy— not me.

My mother came home from work every night. It was almost like it used to be back home, but we didn't go out for dinner every night. Sometimes I started dinner if there was food in the house. Other times, I waited for her to come home to see what she was in the mood for. Sometimes she ate, and sometimes she didn't.

After I finished washing the dinner dishes, there was a knock at the door.

"Hey, JD."

He held out a bouquet of multi colored Gerber daisies. "Uhm, I got these for you. I hope you like them."

I held the flowers to my nose to take their scent in. Turned out, daisies didn't have a scent at all, unlike the peonies we had in our yard back home. We had two big bushes of them. They bloomed huge flowers, and they had the very strong, sweet scent of bergamot. Ants loved them, and because of that, I couldn't bring them inside. I pretended the bushes were big vases holding the flowers for me outside. My neighbor grew Lilly of the Valley flowers. I loved the tiny white bells, no bigger than a thumb nail, that hung down on the stem. They had a sweet smell. I wanted to have these in my bouquet when I got married someday. I loved flowers, and until today, nobody had ever brought me flowers before. Except for when I was in the hospital after my surgery last year, my Grandmother brought me a flower arrangement from a funeral she had been at earlier in the day. I felt very close to Harold, whoever he was.

"Come on in. Uhm, Mom, this is JD. He's in my History and P.E. classes."

"Hi, JD," Mom said.

"Hi, Mrs. Kelly." He said nervously.

"You can call me Mary."

"He brought me flowers. Aren't they pretty?"

"Yes, they are. I can't imagine what you did to deserve those," she said disrespectfully.

My throat tightened as flames stormed into my cheeks.

I couldn't believe she said that to me in front of JD.

"Ah, let's go outside, JD." I closed the door behind me. "I'm sorry, my mom is…"

He stroked my cheek. "Don't worry about it. I thought about you all night when I got home."

We both blushed.

* * *

Monday after school, I was walking home alone. A white Lexus SUV did a U-turn in the road and drove over the sidewalk in front of me. I jumped back before it stopped. The tinted driver's-side window lowered.

"Oh, were you afraid I was going to run you over, you boyfriend stealer?" Jessica shouted.

"Well, I can see why JD didn't want to go out with you anymore. He didn't want to die."

"You aren't very funny, Sandy."

"Whatever, Jessica."

"You had no right taking him from me. He'll get bored with you and come back to me, you'll see."

"Aren't you going to be late for Cheer practice?"

She checked her watch.

"I'll let JD know you said "Hi."

"YOU ARE SUCH A BITCH!" She reversed her car back on the road. Her tires spit up gravel from the shoulder.

EIGHT

Capricorns need escape rooms

A storm blew in the next night JD picked me up. His wipers thumped across the windshield, swishing the rain off as we drove to the rec center. We met Jason and Clarissa in the game room, where there were ping pong tables, pool tables, foosball tables, and pinball machines. Most of the tables and machines were in use. The foosball table was open, so we played guys against girls. Clarissa and I lost all three games, which made the guys very happy. They were so competitive. After the game, we sat and talked in the lounge area while we waited for the weather to clear.

"Hey, guys, tickets for homecoming go on sale next week. Are we in?" Jason asked.

"Sandy, we're going to Homecoming, right?"

"Of course," I said.

"Yeah, girl, let's go dress shopping this weekend. JD, you're in charge of getting the limo, and Jason, you're in charge of you-know-what," Clarissa said.

"Make sure it's a white stretch, JD. And what's our poison for the night?" Jason asked.

"Whatever you can get from your dad's liquor cabinet," JD said.

"I'll get us something good," Jason said.

Clarissa peered out the window. "I think the rain stopped."

"Let's roll, Clarissa," Jason said.

"See you guys later."

Once we got inside JD's car, he opened the glove compartment and handed me a small box. "Do you want to wear my class ring?"

I held his ring in my hand. A football was engraved on one side, and a basketball and baseball were engraved on the other. A large shiny topaz stone was set in the middle.

I handed it back to him. "No, this is yours, you should wear it."

"All right, do you want to wear my ID bracelet?"

"The one you have from the seventh grade with your name on it?" I giggled. "Do you still have one?"

"I'm sure I have it somewhere." He chuckled.

"No, I don't want to wear your ID bracelet. Don't be offended. I just don't want to wear any rings or bracelets making me feel like I'm branded."

"What does that mean?" he asked.

"It means I don't need to wear your jewelry to show I'm your girlfriend. Everyone knows we're going out, and I don't need to prove it by wearing anything. It has nothing to do with you. It's just the way I am."

He put the ring box back in the glove box and closed it. "Most girls want to wear their boyfriend's ring."

"Trust me, I'm not like other girls," I said.

"I know, that's why I like you so much."

"I like you too, JDog."

* * *

Clarissa came to my house before Homecoming. She brought her mother's rollers. I sprayed her hair with water and a little hairspray and wound her hair around the rollers. My hair had a little curl if I didn't blow dry it straight. All I needed to do was twist my hair and hold it in place for twenty minutes before spraying it.

"Show me your dress," Clarissa said.

I pulled the dress from my closet. "I'm glad I packed this. I didn't know if I would need it or not." I removed the plastic and held it up. "I wore this last year at Homecoming."

"Oh, I like the short dress, and I love the royal blue and gold."

I rolled the rest of her hair. "What dress are you wearing?"

"I'm wearing a long dark maroon dress. What color shoes are you wearing?"

I pulled my silver heels out of the closet. "I know they don't match the gold or blue, but I like them."

"Yeah, I love the sparkly silver. You're going to look so nice."

"Thanks. Hey, Clarissa," I hesitated.

"Yes?"

"Why doesn't Jason like me?"

"What? He likes you."

"He doesn't act like it. I don't think he likes that JD and I are going out."

"That's just Jason. He wants to make sure you're not going to hurt his best friend."

"JD?"

"Yep. Those two are very tight. They do everything together and they always watch out for each other."

"I didn't know guys talked about stuff like that."

"Jason tells me everything. You'd be surprised what guys talk about. They have the same feelings we do."

Then why don't they ever show it? Or am I totally missing it? Are their feelings hidden in their words or how they act and don't want us to know? I want someone to come out a say how they feel. I'm not a mind reader. But, I'm not sure I would tell them how I feel either.

"What color eye shadow do you want?"

Clarissa rummaged through my eye shadows. "Uhm, I'll try the light pink. Do you miss Chicago?"

I brushed the shadow over her eyelids. "Yeah. I miss my friends. But, I'm glad I'm here now. Part of me wanted to get away. I didn't want to see *him*..."

"Him?" Clarissa asked.

I fumbled with the eye shadow brush, dropping it on the floor. "He's this boy...I was only ten...He was in my fifth-grade class...he followed me home from school one day and pushed me to the ground. He pinned my arms beneath me and shoved his hand up my shirt and ripped it off."

"Oh my god."

I took a deep breath. It didn't help my shaking hands. "I tried everything to get him off me. But the more I fought, the harder he pushed himself onto me, grinding my hands into the cement, punching me over and over."

"What happen then?"

"When he finally got off me and I ran home crying, my mom was home for lunch. She saw my ripped shirt. I thought she was going to be mad at me."

"Oh my God, what did she do?"

"She called the police and after work we met them at his house. I had to sit in his kitchen while everyone talked about what he did. I fucking hated that."

"Then what happened?"

"Nothing."

"NOTHING?"

"Nope. The police just said "Boys will be boys."

"That is so fucking wrong. They should have done something."

"I don't think it would have mattered. I never told anyone because nobody believes the girl."

"Well, I do. I'm glad you told me. You didn't tell your friends either?"

"No. I didn't tell them either because I was sure he would have denied it. All my friends talked about how great he was in football, wrestling, and baseball. I didn't want my friends to have to decide who was telling the truth and pick sides. So, I said nothing. I kept my mouth shut, but I wanted to kicked him in the balls every time I saw him. I've always wondered if he did this to anyone else."

"I'm so sorry that happened to you."

"I'm okay."

I kept telling myself.

Clarissa and I had become good friends mainly because of JD and Jason. Girls like her were usually out of my league but she excepted me.

"I'm intrigued by the stories you tell about your mom." Is she really like that?"

"Yeah. I haven't even told you everything either. Enough about my past. Tonight is supposed to be fun," I said.

"I can't top your mom but my dad is a well-known heart surgeon in Denver. He isn't home very often. But my mother is home every day. I wish she would get a job or at least a life of her own. She's constantly asking me, "How's your day? Did you get a 'A' on your Algebra test?" And my dad just asks "What University are you applying too?" I feel like I should have flash cards ready and hold them up when they ask me the same questions over and over again. And most likely they wouldn't even notice the same daily replies."

At least she had someone who cared.

It sounded like Clarissa's life had been mapped out since she was born. And she went along with the game plan. I'd heard of girls like her who, after High School or College, veered their parents chosen path. They tried to find themselves by backpacking cross country, exploring the European lifestyle, or somewhere on another planet through drugs. Everyone would have that day. Some came earlier in life and others later. I thought my mother's started on that September day when I came home from school and she said she was leaving. I wondered when my day will be?

'Time to take your curlers out," I said.

Her hair fell into bouncy curls. After she left, I held my dress in front of me and danced in front of the mirror in my room.

* * *

At six p.m. the limo driver picked me up and took me to JD's house. I sat alone in the car and pretended I was a movie star, or at least someone special, for the short ride.

Jason and Clarissa met us at JD's house, where JD's mother proceeded to take countless pictures. "You kids behave yourselves. I don't want any phone calls from jail tonight," JD's mom said.

"Don't worry, Mom. And don't wait up for us either," JD said.

"We'll be cool, Mrs. M," Jason said.

On the way to the Breckenridge Hotel and Convention Center, Jason pulled a bottle of tequila from his backpack. "Yeah, baby." He snapped the cap off the bottle, took a swig, and handed it over to Clarissa.

She held her nose and tipped her head back. Gold liquid flowed from the bottle into her mouth. "This is nice." She handed the bottle to JD.

JD took a long pull. "You did good tonight, Jason," JD wiped his mouth and handed the bottle to me. "You'll like this, Sandy."

"Got any limes in your pocket?" I asked Jason.

"Sorry, Chicago, no limes, but you can check if you want to." He lifted his hips off the seat and pulled the insides of his pockets out.

I shook my head. "No, thanks, I'll pass."

I wasn't a fan of tequila, but I wasn't going to be a party pooper tonight. I sat forward, brought the bottle to my lips, and took a drink. The gold liquid burned my lips, the inside of my mouth, and then my throat.

"Whoa, that's hot. I think my ears are burning. Are they red?" I asked.

"No, they aren't red," JD laughed.

I fell back into the seat. My body softened next to JD's.

The tequila bottle made the rounds until we pulled up to the front of the hotel. The limo driver got out and opened the doors for us. The tequila had gone to my head. I was a little wobbly.

JD wrapped his arm around my waist. "I gotcha, girl."

Jason was the last one out. He handed the half-empty bottle to the driver. "Save it. We'll be back."

The banquet room was decorated in Summit schools' colors of green and white. Tables of ten were set up around the dance floor. A sparkling disco ball hung from the ceiling in the middle of the room.

After a lukewarm sirloin dinner, Jason put his hand on JD's shoulder.

"Yo, JD, remember that time when we got arrested by the five-oh after we drove up on old man Elmer's lawn and ran over his flowerpots? Man, we were totally trashed that night."

"Really? You did that?" I asked.

JD shifted in his chair. "Yeah. We were young and dumb."

"How much trouble did you guys get in?" I asked.

"Not much, our dads got us off. We had to pay to have his lawn fixed and buy new flowerpots," Jason answered. "And what about that time we got hauled down to the police station for smoking pot behind Sam's Fish Market?"

"Oh my god, you guys could have gotten kicked out of school," I said.

"Yep, they could have, but daddy bailed them out—again." Clarissa chimed in.

"We were almost goners," Jason said.

"It's kind of nice having dads who can get you out of trouble, isn't it, boys?" Clarissa said sarcastically.

"C--"

"Stop, Jason," Clarissa said.

JD cleared his throat. "Jason, man, let's talk about something else."

"Yeah, let's go dance, guys," Clarissa said.

Clarissa pulled Jason onto the dance floor by his shirt collar. JD and I followed. We passed Jessica sitting at a table with her cheer friends.

"Bitch," she sneered at me.

JD stopped. "Jessica..."

"No, don't," I said, tugging his arm.

"I'm not going to let her talk to you that way," JD said.

"It doesn't matter. She's not worth it."

"You got something to say to me, JD," Jessica sassed back.

JD pointed at Jessica. I pulled him away. "Let's go, JD."

"What was that all about?" Clarissa asked.

"Nothing. It's just Jessica being Jessica," I said.

"She has no right to call you that," JD said.

"I don't care what she says or anyone else. I know what I am and what I'm not."

"But, still…"

"No more. We're here to have fun, keep dancing." I rested my head on his chest. I glanced over at Jessica and smiled.

The dance ended at midnight. Our limo was out front. JD and Jason sprinted toward it. When they got to the car, the driver opened the door. "Gentlemen, how was your evening?" the limo driver asked.

"Good, good." JD and Jason both answered together. They jumped inside and searched for the bottle.

The driver bent down and peered in at them. "Sorry, guys, it's gone. Can't leave open liquor in the car," he slurred, reeking of tequila.

"Damn." They echoed each other again.

"This should be a fun ride home. Sandy, slide over here and hang on to me," JD said.

We made it to Jason's house safe and sound. Except the limo driver hit the curb parking in front of Jason's house. Jason held the door for Clarissa. "Catch you guys later," Jason said.

The driver lowered the window to the back. "Where to next?"

"Do you have to go home?" JD asked me.

"No. I can stay out."

"Take us to my house," JD told the driver.

A few minutes later, the limo driver pulled up to JD's house.

JD took my hand. We crept quietly into his house and down to the family room. "What do you want to watch?" JD whispered, fumbling with the TV remote.

"I don't know. What's on at this hour?" I whispered back.

"Ah, it doesn't matter, we won't be watching it anyway." He tossed the remote on the chair. "Come here, girl."

JD and I made out for a while on the couch. It was a lot easier than in the backseat of JD's car. We undressed each other. I gave JD a back massage, and then JD massaged my body. He started with his hands and finished with his lips. I wasn't sure who fell asleep first, but it was probably me.

I woke up to an angry voice coming from upstairs. "John, you need to talk to your son now! Did you know JD and Sandy were downstairs last night? They're practically naked, laying on top of each other on the couch," JD's mom yelled.

Our clothes were draped over the chair across the room.

"JD!" His dad yelled downstairs.

I nudged JD. "You better go up there. Your parents sound pretty mad."

JD hesitantly got up, holding his head in his hands. "Damn it." He pulled his pants on, and stomped upstairs. I heard his mother again.

"JD, what were you thinking having Sandy spend the night here without even asking?"

"I didn't think it would be a problem, my friends stay over all the time. All we did was watch movies, and I guess we fell asleep."

I closed my eyes.

I think I just got JD in trouble.

"JD, girls don't spend the night like your buddies do, and you know it. And I better not find you two in your bed one of these days. Are you listening to me?"

"Relax, Mom, it's not what you think," JD said.

"Don't tell me to relax, young man, and I know what I saw: you and Sandy with no clothes, on the couch, practically on top of each other," she said firmly. "So, what *should* I be thinking, John David?"

I pulled the blanket over my head.

What? JD's name is really John David?

"I give up. You talk to him, John," his mom said.

"JD, it's time to take Sandy home, and when you get back, we will continue this talk, understand?" his father said calmly.

"I told you nothing happened. All we did was fall asleep," JD yelled back at his dad.

I heard someone stomping down the stairs. My heart raced.

Please be JD.

I poked my head out to see who it was. I sighed in relief and lifted the blanket off my head, wrapping it around me. "I heard," I said.

JD handed me my dress and shoes. "Let's go. I have to take you home."

I dressed quickly. We drove to my house in silence.

* * *

Later that night, JD called me before bed.

"Did your mom say anything more to you when you got home?" I asked.

"No, she wasn't home when I got back."

"What did your dad say?"

"Office—now. I guess they didn't buy that all we did was watch movies."

"Yeah, the fact we were both in our underwear didn't help much," I said.

"It was so nice having you in my arms all night," JD said.

Having JD next to me last night was nice. It made me feel safe. I hated sleeping alone in my house every night.

"Yeah, it was nice. So, what did your Dad say to you?"

"First, he told me, 'You gave your mom a heart attack." JD laughed. "She's so paranoid. And having a lawyer for a dad, nothing ever gets past him. I wanted to plead the Fifth, but I didn't think he'd find it very funny."

"Ha, I'm sure he wouldn't."

"I was hoping he wouldn't give me a lie detector test."

"Would you have passed?"

"Probably not. He also told me he was worried we're getting too close too fast. He told me he didn't want me to *throw* my future away on some girl."

My heart sank. "What does that mean? He thinks by going out with me, you'll be throwing your future away?" I asked.

I'm not just some girl!

I wrapped my blanket around me. Maybe my mom was right, I wasn't good enough for anyone.

"No. I'm not sure, but he asked if I was using protection."

"Why? We weren't doing anything."

"I know. I told him nothing happened last night. Then he started interrogating me about sex and if we were doing it and if I'd done it with anyone else."

"And what did you tell him?"

"Well, yeah, when I was with Jessica, but not with you," JD said.

I hated hearing Jessica's name. I knew he slept with her, but I still didn't want to hear about it. What was he even thinking, going out with her, anyway? And she was a total bitch for calling me a bitch every time she saw me.

"Sounds like your dad's paranoid, too," I said.

"Yep. Uhm, maybe we should talk about this, too."

"About what?"

"Are you on birth control?" JD asked.

I closed my eyes. My stomach rose into my chest. "No. I didn't see a need for it if I wasn't sleeping with anyone."

"Someday, you might. I mean, we will. Don't you think?"

"Yeah, I'll think about it." My stomach knotted.

But not today.

"I've got to go, I'll talk to you tomorrow," I said.

"Yeah, alright, I'll see you tomorrow."

NINE

Capricorns never give up

After talking to JD, I called Clarissa. I paced the floor. "Hey, Clarissa, it's Sandy."

"What's up?"

"Ah, uhm…"

"Say it, girl, what's up?"

"Ah, I need to talk to someone about— birth control."

"Is that all? Jeez, I thought you were going to tell me something bad. Can't you talk to your mom?"

Are you kidding me?

My throat clenched. "No, I can't talk to her about this."

"Then, if I were you, I'd go to the free clinic in town. They can help you. Do you want me to go with you?" She asked.

"Ah, no, I'm good. I can go by myself."

"I'd go soon, before…

"I will. I wouldn't let that happen. Oh, and don't say anything to anyone," I said.

"I won't, but, girl, it's about time."

"Yeah, I guess."

"Call me later if you want," she said.

"Yeah, all right." I walked to my mirror.

Mirror, mirror on the wall, who's the biggest virgin of them all?

Me, I guess. I didn't want to be the only senior who was still a virgin.

I want my first time to be special. I don't want to be squished in JD's back seat.

I want rose petals surrounding me, birds chirping, waves crashing.

Who am I kidding—back seat, here I come.

* * *

A couple of days later, I took the bus to the clinic.

"Do you have an appointment?" The receptionist asked me. I shook my head. She handed me a number and told me to have a seat. They would call me when they were ready. I thumbed through used magazines, trying to avoid eye contact with other girls and a very pregnant woman.

The waiting room was empty when a nurse opened the door and called my number. "Number 42."

I was the only one left. I was number 42. My throat went dry.

"I'm number 42."

Inside the exam room was a chair, a stool on wheels, and a couple of cabinets. The exam table had metal stirrups at one end. The nurse took my name, address, phone number, and previous medical information.

"What brings you in today, Sandy?"

"Ah, I'd like birth control pills," I said nervously.

"I will let the doctor know." She handed me a large paper napkin. "Take all your clothes off, wrap this around you, and have a seat up on the exam table. The Doctor will be in shortly." Before she shut the door, she said, "I can come in with the doctor. if you'd like."

"Okay."

I took everything off. My butt crunched on the paper when I sat on the exam table. A few minutes later, the doctor and nurse walked in. "I'm Dr. Sarah," she said. "The nurse told me you are here for birth control."

"Yes."

"Have you had an internal exam before?" The doctor asked.

"Uhm, no."

"Don't be nervous. Nothing I do today will hurt you. How sexually active are you?"

My eyes glazed over. "Ah…"

"How often do you have sexual intercourse?"

The nurse adjusted the stirrups and spread metal objects on the tray next to the table. I listened to the doctor but kept my eyes on the nurse. "Uhm, I haven't yet. But I want to make sure when I do, nothing will happen."

The doctor reviewed my chart. She ran a gloved finger across my scar and asked about my surgery. "Your scar should fade in a couple of years." She checked my eyes, ears, and throat, before listening to my heart.

All of this for some pills? What kind were they?

When she was done, she told me to scoot my bottom to the end of the table and lie back. I thought I was going to fall off the table. The doctor sat at the end of the table. The nurse placed my feet in the stirrups and told me to relax my legs. The doctor turned a bright light on and disappeared under the paper napkin. I stared at the ceiling and counted the tiles until something very cold and hard entered me. I tensed.

The nurse put her hand on my stomach. "Try and relax, Sandy. You're almost done."

I closed my eyes and held my breath. I was no longer counting the ceiling tiles.

After my exam, the nurse helped me slide back on the table and left the room. I pulled the paper napkin over me.

"Everything looks good," the doctor said. "I think birth control pills will be a good fit for you. It will help regulate your cycle too. There are side effects. Possible weight gain, water retention. Breast swelling or tenderness. Upset stomach and mood changes. They can also help with period cramps, and of course prevent pregnancy if they are taken correctly."

"How much are they?"

"Do you have insurance?"

"Uhm, my insurance is through my dad's work. Will he have to know about this?"

"He may or may not find out. He is entitled to know about all claims on his insurance, though. We can bill your dad's insurance for your exam and if you don't have any money, we give you the pills for free. Okay?"

"Yeah."

"I'll send the nurse back in with them," she said and left.

A few minutes later the nurse came back. "Okay, Miss Sandy, here is your first pack of pills. Take one every day, and don't forget. Read the instructions on the pamphlet inside. You can pick up a new pack every month. If you have any questions, call the office." She left the room.

I opened the pack. Twenty-one white pills and seven pink pills lined up in a dial held by silver foil. I already felt different just having birth control pills in my hand, like someone was giving me permission to have sex: "Here you go, now go ahead and do it." I didn't want to change. I was happy with who I was, but I knew I would change after this. Maybe I should have done what Jason said and just gone for it.

Eww, why was I thinking about Jason?

I wondered, now that I was taking these if I would still be able to say No. It was too much to think about, so many scenarios swirled in my head.

I guess I'm doing this. Get ready, JD.

I pushed a pill out, swallowed it, and got dressed.

TEN

Don't try to understand a Capricorn

It was an unusually warm night in November. After JD's basketball game, JD, Jason, Clarissa, and I headed to the batting cages behind the rec center. Jamison and Tammy followed us in their car.

After we parked, the guys grabbed their baseball bats and helmets from behind the back seat of JD's Jeep. Both bats were silver metal Easton Ghost Evolutions. JD's had blue tape wrapped around the handle, and Jason's bat had red tape. Jamison preferred a wood batt wrapped with black tape. Inside the batting cage, Jason filled the pitching machine with baseballs he purchased inside.

JD placed a helmet on my head. "Here, I don't want you to hurt your pretty little head."

"JD, man, you're going to make me barf. Quit with the lovey-dovey stuff," Jason said.

"I think it's nice," Clarissa said. "It wouldn't hurt you to say nice things like that to me, would it?"

Jason shook his head. "Who's hitting first?"

"I'll go first," Jamison said. He grabbed his bat and stood at the inground home plate.

Jason flipped the red metal switch on the fence post to start the ball machine.

JD and I sat on the bench next to Clarissa and Tammy and watched Jamison hit several balls.

When he was done batting, he yelled to Jason, "You're up."

Jamison and Jason switched places.

"JD, why are there lights on at the ski resort?" I asked.

"They're getting everything set up for snow season, which should have started already," he said.

"The slopes are so pretty, even with no snow on them," I said.

"Hey, Chicago, what are you doing after graduation?" Jason asked. He swung his bat, connecting with the first pitch.

"Yeah? What are you doing, Sandy?" JD asked.

"I don't know. Why? What are you going to do, JD?"

"I'm going to CU in Boulder. I got a partial scholarship for baseball."

"Nice, JD. Well deserved," Jamison yelled over to him.

"What are you going to study, JD?" Tammy asked.

"Architecture," JD said.

"Architecture? Really?" I asked. "Have you gone on the architecture tour in Chicago along the Chicago River?"

"No, I haven't. Is it any good?" JD asked.

"Yeah. Chicago has great architectural buildings that were built after the great Chicago fire in 1871. Haven't you heard the legend of Mrs. O'Leary's cow?"

"Can't say that I have."

"Well, rumor has it one of her cows named Daisy tipped over the lantern while she was milking it in the barn. The fire spread so fast it burned the city down. They removed all the damage and rebuilt the city. It's so awesome and beautiful now."

I guess when you find yourself destroyed, you need to clear the wreckage and rebuild.

Jamison patted JD on the back. "It figures an Irishman would burn down a city."

Jason laughed.

"Haha Jamison," JD said.

I continued. "Oh, and did you know they reversed the flow of the Chicago river? It used to flow into Lake Michigan, and now it flows away from the Lake. They changing directions, and the river became useful." I closed my eyes and breathed in my own words. There is a boat tour you can take that tells you the history of everything. It's pretty interesting if you ever get a chance to go to Chicago."

"Have you ever thought about being a tour guide, Sandy?" Jason asked.

"No, Jason, I haven't. So, what are you doing after graduation, Jason?" I asked.

"Texas A&M. I'm thinking about becoming a lawyer like my dad, but I'm not one hundred percent sure yet." He hit a few more balls, knocking them into the outfield net.

I made eye contact with Clarissa. "Are you going away, too, Clarissa?"

"Yep, I'm going to AU in Phoenix. I want to be a pharmacist."

Jason hit another ball, which fowled away. "Nice, now I know where I can get my drugs if I need them."

"Ah, only the legal drugs, Jason," Clarissa said.

Jamison sat on the bench next to us.

"Where are you going, Jamison?" I asked.

"I'm joining the Navy after graduation. I want to kick ass and take names."

JD and Jason saluted their friend. A ball shot out, almost hitting Jason.

A little smile crossed my lips.

So close, but yet so far.

"Damn, that ball almost hit me," Jason yelled out. "Who's next?"

JD picked up his bat. "I'll go. I'll show you guys how it's done."

"Tammy, what about you?" I asked.

"I'll probably get my associate's degree in business and work for my dad at his insurance company."

"That's pretty cool, having a ready-made job," I said.

"So, Sandy, why don't you know what you want to do yet?" Clarissa asked.

"I don't know. I haven't thought about it."

JD connected with every ball, sending them flying into the dark night. I felt like one of those balls--flying off into the future with no clue where I'd land.

"That was a homerun, JD," Jason said.

The ball sailed out of sight. "It sure was," he said. He rested his bat against the fence.

"Sandy, you're not going back home after graduation, are you?" JD asked.

"No. Well, I don't know," I said.

"Well, I don't want you to leave," JD said.

"Oh, that's so sweet, JD," Jason teased.

"Shut up," JD slapped at Jason.

"I guess I'd like to go to cosmetology school and then go from there," I said.

"Why not CU?" JD asked.

"I can't afford it, JD." I kicked a ball into the fence.

"You can get a loan or something," Tammy said. "That's what I'm doing. And if I pass all my classes and graduate on time my dad told me he'd pay off my loan."

"Yeah, that won't happen with my parents. I'm on my own from now on," I said.

"I think you should be a cosmetologist. I loved how you did my hair and makeup for Homecoming. You'd be so good at it, too. I'm sure there's a cosmetology school somewhere out here. And I'll bet there's one in Boulder, too," Clarissa offered.

My heart warmed. "Thanks, Clarissa. That's so nice of you. I need to start looking."

"Ha! You'll be a beauty school dropout, like Frenchie in *Grease. Beauty school dropout...*" Jason sang.

I rolled my eyes. "Very funny, Jason."

First, I was born Sandy, and now I was Frenchie. Maybe next I'd be Rizzo, the Leader of the Pink Ladies. She didn't take any shit from anyone.

"Jason, who sings that song?" Clarissa asked.

"Frankie Avalon, why?"

"I think you should let him sing it, then," Clarissa teased.

"Haha," Jason said.

"Or you could always join the military, Sandy," Jamison interjected.

"No! Don't even say that, Jamison. She will not be joining the military," JD said.

"Enough chatter. Let's get down to business," Jason said.

He pulled a bottle of Jack Daniels out of his backpack.

"Humm, maybe I'll open a liquor store, so Jason will have a place to buy all his booze. I'd be a millionaire," I said.

"No, you wouldn't. You'd go broke because Jason would expect it to be free," JD joked.

"Jason, where do you get all your liquor from anyway?" I asked.

"My dad's liquor cabinet. He hasn't missed any yet so far." He twisted the cap off and waived it around. "Now, who's first?" he asked.

JD and Jamison both raised their hands and said, "me, me."

Jason extended his arm toward JD and then pulled the bottle back. "Sorry, dude, I'm first."

Jason took a long pull on the bottle. As he swallowed, he shook his head back and forth like a wet dog shaking water off it's back. "This shit's wicked." He wiped his mouth with the back of his hand and handed the bottle to Clarissa.

Her lips covered the top and she filled her mouth. After she swallowed her eyes opened wide as the burning sensation hit her. "Holy shit," she said.

Jason kissed her. "Way to swallow, C. I knew there was a reason why I loved you."

"Oh, Jason, Jason, Jason," JD chuckled.

Clarissa held the bottle out to JD. He gulped the burning liquid down hard with no problem and handed the bottle to me.

"This is gonna kill me," I said.

"Hold your nose and don't think about it," Clarissa said.

I pinched my nose and raised the bottle to my lips. JD lifted the bottom of the bottle, filling my mouth even more.

Thanks, JD.

The hot liquid burned the inside of my mouth. I was afraid to swallow. It was like fire water.

JD and Jason laughed and chanted. "Swallow, swallow, swallow."

Ugh, here it goes.

I closed my eyes and relaxed my throat, letting it slip down. It burned all the way to my stomach.

This was worse than the tequila.

"I want you all to know I am not a professional whiskey drinker," I said.

"You're up, Sandy," JD said, handing me the bat. "Keep your eye on the ball."

"I want you all to know I am not a professional baseball player, either."

"Just hit the ball, Chicago," Jason said.

I held the bat high above my head and then dropped my shoulder. I swung and missed. "I quit. Who's next?" I asked.

"JD, do you see who's over at the other cage?" Jason asked.

"No, who? Carrillo? Who's he with?"

"Looks like his brothers." Jamison said.

"I hate that guy," JD said.

"Why do you hate him?" I asked.

"It's a long, long story," Jason snickered.

"Yeah, you don't want to know. Too much history," Clarissa said.

"More like bad history," Tammy said.

"He's a douche," JD added.

"I think we're done," Jamison said, picking up his bat. "Are you guys ready to go?"

"Yeah, I think we're going to go, too," Jason said.

"Sandy and I are going to stay awhile longer," JD said.

"You and Clarissa can ride with us," Jamison said.

After everyone left, JD came around behind me and positioned the bat in my hands. He turned my hips and lifted my right elbow slightly. "Now, this is how you hold the bat."

"Hey, McCarron, how's it going?" Tom asked from outside the fence.

"We're good, Tom. You can leave now," JD said.

"Oh, hey, didn't I see you playing tennis with Coach Dan last week?" Tom asked.

"Yeah, I remember meeting you," I said.

"We're kind of busy right now, Tom." JD said, turning away from him.

"I've got to get going, too. Maybe I'll see you around town," Tom said.

"Don't count on it," JD replied.

"I wasn't talking about you, McCarron. I was talking about her." Tom nodded in my direction and walked away.

JD walked toward the gate but then backed away and came up behind me again. "Now, where were we before we were so rudely interrupted?"

"I think you were holding me like this," I said, wrapping his arms around my waist.

"I hope you don't think I was a jerk telling you you aren't joining the military."

"I don't, but I have no idea what I want to do. Neither of my parents will pay for school, so I have to figure it out on my own."

"I…don't want you to leave, and if you do leave…" He sighed, "I'd be lost without you."

"Let's not talk about this anymore," I said.

I took my helmet off and sat on the bench. "So, where do you guys go skinny-dipping out here?"

JD arched his eyebrows. "What? Skinny dipping?"

"Yeah, don't you guys have a lake or a pond to go skinny-dipping here?"

"No. The water in every lake comes from the mountains. It's ice cold. You won't be jumping in anywhere in Colorado without clothes on."

"That's a bummer. Back home, me and my friends went skinny-dipping almost every night in the summer. I'm going to miss that."

"You're going to miss getting naked with the guys, huh?"

"No, it's not like that. And it isn't about getting naked either. It's fun and liberating," I said.

"Yeah, yeah, yeah," JD teased.

"Whatever," I elbowed him in the ribs as he sat down next to me. "Anyway, we'd go swimming at a pig farm that had a water hole. A couple times, the owner came out and shot rock salt at us. Man, that salt burned when it hit you…but we still went back. So then the farmer started dumping pig shit in the water to keep us out. I hated that guy."

JD shook his head and laughed. "Sounds like you and your friends were a bunch of troublemakers."

"Ha! Speaking of troublemakers…"

"No, we are not going to talk about that. I'm not that guy anymore." JD said.

He took my hands in his. We tilted our heads back and watched the stars flicker on and off as clouds slowly floated by.

"Oh…oh! JD, up in the sky, did you see that?"

"Yeah, a shooting star. That was a long one. Must have come from far away."

"Make a wish, make a wish. But don't tell me what it is," I said.

"If I make a wish, do you think my wish will come true?" He asked.

"I don't know. It's supposed to. Why? What did you wish for?"

"I'm not telling. Remember, you told me not to tell."

JD kissed the back of my neck and stood, pulling me up with him.

"Let's forget about everything tonight," he whispered.

The moonlight followed us back to his Jeep.

"I've got a surprise for you," JD said, navigating out of the parking lot into the darkness.

"What?"

"You'll see." He drove toward his house.

He parked in front of a neighbor's house and killed the engine.

"Why are you parking here?" I asked.

"So my parents won't know I'm home. Don't worry, we're not going in the house. We're going in the hot tub," he said.

"Ah…"

"You said you wanted to go skinny-dipping…didn't you?"

JD took my hand. We crept around the backyard and into the hot tub pagoda. "I don't see any lights on. Hopefully, they're asleep."

Ah, yeah, I hope they're asleep too. I don't want another scene like Homecoming.

He removed the cover and turned the hot tub up to 100 degrees. Steam from the hot water rose in the cool air and blanketed the windows. He pressed the power button on. The water bubbled and swirled. A scent of chlorine touched my nose.

"Ready?" JD asked as he took his clothes off, leaving only his boxers on, and climbed into the water. I told him to turn around, then I took off my clothes. As I stepped into the tub, the bubbles engulfed my body with warmth, easing me into relaxation. JD immediately pulled me to him. His hands found my waist, then lower, he raised his eyebrows and a crooked smile flashed on his face. *Yes, JD*, I was completely naked.

"Nice, I think I'll join you. I don't want to be overdressed." He removed his boxers, and threw them over his head onto the deck. I straddled his lap. He held me in his arms, and we started kissing. My heart raced.

This was really going to happen.

I dropped my hand down between his legs, took hold of his dick, and guided it between my thighs, hoping he'd get the message.

Still holding my ass in his hands, he quietly asked, "Really?"

I nodded. "I'm ready, JDog."

His hands caressed my face. Water trailed from them, running down my face and dripping onto my breasts, before mixing in the hot tub. "Are you sure about this?"

I nodded.

"So, you trust me now, right?"

My voice quivered a little. "Yes. I am so ready for you now."

I felt a little empowered, having prepared myself. And I had my armor, my pills.

"Uhm, are you…"

"Yes, taken care of." Those little pills were my precaution, and they better do their job. I glanced over at his clothes, thinking he should have a condom, but JD's hand directed my attention back to him.

Don't suppose it matters. We're in a hot tub.

He kissed my forehead, then started kissing my neck and then down to my shoulders. The lower he went, the harder he pressed his lips into me. I felt him position himself between my thighs and then he slid slowly inside me.

"Are you okay?" he asked.

I nodded.

"Girl, talk to me. I need to hear you say it," he said.

"Yes, I'm ready. Just go slow."

JD pushed himself inside.

"Am I doing it right?" I asked.

"Don't worry about anything right now. Hold on to me, and let me take you there."

He gripped my hips and raised them up and down. I held on to him and buried my face in his neck. I wondered if it was meant to be uncomfortable. I tried to enjoy the moment. He held the back of my head with his hands tangled in my wet hair. I found myself breathing heavily with every movement. He tipped my head back and watched me with every thrust. Our bodies became one. I was being held while warm water wrapped around me. I wanted this feeling of closeness with JD to last forever, but then he finished. He squeezed my hips, and I hoped he would keep going…but he slid me over to his side.

The water in the hot tub was still rolling long after we'd stopped to catch our breath. JD kissed me softly on the lips.

"Are you okay?"

My mind was empty, I tried to think, and then I blurted out the only thing that popped in my head: "Oh, my god, why did I wait so long?"

JD threw his head back and laughed.

I wondered if this was his wish.

ELEVEN

Capricorns like making improvements around the house

The next morning, I woke up to the phone ringing. I picked it up.

"Good morning. How are you feeling today?" JD asked.

"I'm good. How about *you*?"

"I'm more than good. Last night was amazing," he said.

I closed my eyes, picturing JD holding me. That feeling would never be shared again with anyone. "I know. I was still in bed thinking about it. Is that wrong?"

"No, not at all." He laughed. "Have you looked outside yet? There's a ton of snow on the ground."

I rolled out of bed, shuffled to the window, and opened the curtains. Glistening white snow covered the trees. Peaks of snow nestled on the window ledge. Snow drifts blanketed the grass and parking lot.

So, this was what a Breckenridge snowfall looked like. I wondered how many inches fell last night.

Thank God I didn't have to shovel snow anymore.

"Wow, it's so pretty," I said.

"Yeah, the first real snow of the season. Ahh, you're not going to like this, but my parents know about last night."

My stomach dropped. "What about last night?" I asked.

"About us, in the hot tub."

I turned away from the window. "How?"

"We have a motion-sensor security system, and I guess when we were in the hot tub, the camera came on and started recording…"

"What?"

"Yeah, they heard everything," JD said.

My heart dropped into my empty stomach. I climbed back into bed and pulled the blankets over my head.

"Oh, my god, JD. What did they hear? What did they see? What did they say?"

"Well, my mom acted like she didn't know anything at first, but then she sarcastically asked 'how did you sleep last night, JD?' When I told her I slept fine, she smirked and said, 'I'm sure you did.' "Then my dad said, 'Good morning, JDog.' He's never called me that before, and I don't think he's ever heard you call me JDog before."

"Ah…and then?"

"He said, 'I hope you don't have plans today because you'll be cleaning the hot tub.' I almost pissed my pants when he mentioned the hot tub. I should have told him fine and dropped it, but I asked him why I had to clean it since nobody ever used it."

"And then," I said.

"Then, he showed me the red flashing light on the security system by the back door. I swear to you, I didn't know there was an alarm and a camera that turned on when someone entered the hot tub… the camera recorded everything."

"JD, you're joking, right?"

"I wish I was," he said.

"They saw everything?" I shrieked, sitting up and kicking the blankets off.

"No, it was too dark. They could only hear us..."

"What? They heard everything? I mean, they didn't turn it off when they heard what...what we were doing?"

"Yeah, I guess not," JD said.

"You guess what? That they turned it off or kept listening?" I asked.

"I don't know. I really didn't want to get into the details, if you know what I mean. I wasn't exactly looking for a thumbs-up."

"That's not funny, JD!" I jumped out of bed and paced the cold wood floor.

"I know, but there's nothing I can do about it now."

I yanked my fingers through my dry tangled hair. "What else did they say?"

"My mom was pretty mad. She started in again saying, 'Honestly, JD, what were you thinking?' Then she told my father he'd better have *another* talk with me."

"Oh crap," I sat on my bed and tucked my knees under my chin. I knotted my fingers even more in my hair.

God, please, this can't be happening.

"Are you still there?" JD asked.

"Yeah, yeah."

"Like always, my dad said, 'office, JD.' *And,* when we got to his office, he started in on me. 'I'm getting tired of having to talk to you about this. This house is *off-limits* to your sexual activities, got it?' Then he yelled at me to get outside and clean the hot tub."

"Now what?" I asked.

"I guess I'll be freezing my ass off cleaning the hot tub today...But it was worth it."

The air was silent.

"Sandy, Are you still there?"

"Yeah, I'm thinking. I'd offer to help you, but I think I'll stay away from your house for a while. Call me later?"

"I will…bye."

I jumped off my bed, picked my robe up off the floor, and climbed back into bed. I couldn't dial the phone fast enough.

"Hey, Holly."

"Uhm, are you still a virgin? If you are, I'm hanging up."

Nerves shook my voice. "No…wait…I'm not."

"Oh my god. Tell me everything. Was it with JD? How did it happen? Are you okay?"

She was talking so fast.

Slow down. Slow down.

"Well, yes— it was with JD. We did it in his parents…outdoor hot tub last night. And I'm more than okay."

"What? In a hot tub? Oh my God. Too funny. And…"

"And…what?"

"Tell me all about it."

A smile touched my lips. "It was nice, so different than I thought it would be."

"Of course, you were in a hot tub. Did he buy you anything? Promise to do your homework?"

"Ah, no, nothing like that. But now that you bring it up I should have asked him to write my History paper. Oh well. Are you ready for this?" My stomach fluttered.

"What? What?"

"We were in the hot tub minding our own business and his parents have a security camera that came on when we opened the door and got in the hot tub."

"Oh shit, does that mean you made a porno?"

I shot up out of bed. "What? God, no!" I slumped back on the bed. "Well… it was too dark to see anything, I hope. But his parents heard the whole thing."

"Oh my God, this is so funny."

I held my hand over my face. "I'll never be able to look either of his parents in the eye again."

"Well, at least you have a great first time story to tell."

"I'm not sure I'll be telling anyone else about this. Anyway, we got our first real snow last night. How's the weather there?"

"It's cold as hell, but no snow yet."

"The snow is so different here. It's powder, not the heavy wet crap we get in Chicago."

"Ugh, I'm so jealous."

"I know, I can't wait to go in it. And the best part of living in an apartment is I won't have to shovel it like I did back home. The apartment manager hires people to shovel and plow. So, how's everything with you?"

"Everything's good."

"How's Rusty?"

"He's good, we're good. You still okay with this?"

"Yeah, gosh, don't worry. I'm good. But don't tell him about my hot tub experience. I don't want him teasing me about this for the rest of my life."

"I won't, but you've got to admit, it's pretty darn funny. Let me know when you're going to release your sex tape."

My whole body tensed. "Shut up."

"Well, I gotta go. Rusty just pulled into the driveway. I'll talk to you later."

"Yeah, see ya, Bestie."

I wished she was here in my room talking about every little thing in person, but then again, maybe this conversation was better to have over the phone.

* * *

Monday morning when JD and I got to school, I wondered if anyone could tell I was no longer a virgin. Did I look any different? I didn't feel different. I guess nothing was different. Except JD, who had a stupid smile on his face.

"Stop smiling so much," I said.

"Why? I can't help it." He wrapped his arm around me.

"Yes, you can," I said.

"How about round two after school today?"

"Is that all you want to do now?"

"What do you mean? Don't you want to?" He asked.

"Yeah, but I don't want that to be all our relationship is about now."

"You worry too much. And no, nothing will change, you'll see," he said.

"I know. This is all new to me."

We stopped at my locker and just as I was opening the door, Jessica walked by. JD didn't even acknowledge her. He kissed the back of my hand. Out of the corner of my eye, I tried to see if Jessica was there. She wasn't. We headed to history.

"What are you doing for Thanksgiving?" JD asked.

"Ah, I don't know. Probably nothing." I didn't think the holidays would mean much out here with no homemade pumpkin pie, no family fights, and no sneaking brandy ices behind my grandmothers back. “What are you doing?” I asked.

“We’re going to my uncle’s house in Denver. Come with me,” JD said.

“I don’t think I can.”

“Why not?”

“I don’t want to leave my mom alone.”

“Will she even be home?”

“I think so.”

“All right. But if she’s not going to be home, you’re coming with me. You’re not staying home alone.”

“I’ll talk to her and let you know,” I said.

Thursday, November 22nd.

Late in the afternoon, I laid on the couch, head propped up on a pillow, and watched the skiers on the slopes from my living room window. The hills were packed. Snow swirled off the peaks every time the wind picked up. Gondolas and lifts filled with skiers wearing brightly colored jackets and hats crept up the mountainside. I guess people didn’t celebrate Thanksgiving at home here. Mom was sitting on the couch, reading a True Crime book.

“Mom, when are you going to put the turkey in?”

“We’re not having turkey today,” she said without looking up from her book.

I shuffled into the kitchen and opened the oven. It was empty. “Why not?”

“I’m not going to cook a big dinner for just the two of us.”

“But it’s Thanksgiving. Don’t they have small turkeys?”

“I’m sure they do, but we’re having spaghetti,” mom said.

In the kitchen, a couple of jars of sauce were sitting on the counter. Two pans sat empty on the stove.

"I don't even think the Italians eat spaghetti on Thanksgiving."

"Take it or leave it, Sandy."

I wished I could leave it, but it was too late to go with JD. This would be the first Thanksgiving without turkey and family.

"Are we going home for Christmas?" I asked.

"No, we can't afford to go home, and you know I have to work. I don't get time off like you do."

"Don't you think it would be nice to have family around?"

"I'm trying to read. Go find something to do."

"Whatever. I wish I had a job here like I did back home. I felt stupid not having a birthday gift for JD on his birthday."

"I'm sure he got over it. Besides, I'm sure his parents bought him everything he wanted, anyway. And what could you possibly give him that he doesn't already have?"

I ignored her question.

Uhm, me, for one.

"Do you like living out here better than back home?" I asked.

"Do you like living out here better?" Mom asked.

"I like it, now that I have friends and JD. I was asking because you're not home much. Do you have a boyfriend?"

She closed the book. "You don't need to know everything I do."

"I was curious to see if you found someone special. I guess I want you to be happy."

"I'm fine. Don't you worry about me."

"All right, I won't worry about you. How come you never ask me if I'm happy?"

Her face was hard. "I don't need to. You are responsible for your own happiness."

What the fuck, mom?

"It's Thanksgiving. You're supposed to be thankful for what you have."

"Then be thankful for what you have and that we have food to eat."

I shook my head in disbelief. "When will dinner be ready?" I asked.

"We're going to eat at Five. Oh, and don't go anywhere. Sharon is going to call."

"Who cares," I mumbled under my breath, walking to my room. Nothing had changed from back home. Maybe she was right. I was responsible for my own happiness.

Later that night, JD called me. "Hey, how was your dinner?"

"She made spaghetti," I said.

"No turkey?"

"No, and don't ask."

"Ah, you sound down. What's up?"

"I am down. I talked to my sister today. She told me my cat died."

"What, what happened?"

"He got hit by a car," I said.

"And she was sure it was your cat?"

"Yeah, it was him. He was orange and white, and he had six toes on each foot, so, it was him. Some friends of my sister saw him on the side of the road by Yany's Chicken House."

"What was he doing there?"

"He liked to go there and hang out by the back door when they closed. The girls who worked there would give him chicken."

"Ha…"

"Are you laughing?" I asked.

"No… ah, not really. But I am picturing this orange cat with huge feet running down the street with a chicken leg in his mouth."

"Really, JD?"

"I'm sorry. I hope he died happy."

I was silent.

"Are you still there?"

"Yes," I answered, holding back tears.

"I can get you another cat for Christmas if you want. They have hundreds of them at the shelter."

"No, I can't have a cat here," I said.

"I want you to be happy. If you want another cat, I'll get one for you. You can sneak it in. But, I'm not sure I can find one with six toes on each foot. What was his name anyway?"

"Widget. Let's change the subject. So, how was your dinner?"

"It was good. I stuffed myself," he said.

"It must have been nice having family around."

"It was. I wished you could have come with me. Everyone asked about you."

"What did you say?"

"I told them you are the love of my life."

"Very funny, JD," I said.

"I mean it."

"Do you want to come over?" I asked.

"Is your mom home?"

"Yeah."

"Don't take this the wrong way, but… I don't like your mom. She makes me feel like I'm doing something wrong, or like I'm—"

"I know what you mean. And I don't like the way she treats you either," I said.

"Did she like your other boyfriends?"

"Yeah, but that's because they partied with her. I don't want you anywhere near her."

"Do you think she's jealous?" JD asked.

"Of who?"

"You," he said.

"Why would a mother be jealous of her own daughter?"

"Because you have a nice life and a great boyfriend, and she doesn't."

"I tried asking her if she had a boyfriend tonight."

"Does she?"

"She told me not to worry about her, so, I'm not going to anymore. I can't talk any more. I have to go do the dishes before bed. I'll see you tomorrow."

"Sandy, why do you always change the subject when you don't want to talk?"

"I don't change the subject. And…and it doesn't matter. Talking doesn't change anything."

Why does JD have to point out everything I do wrong? "I have to go. Good night, JD."

"All right, talk to you tomorrow. Hey…"

"What?"

"Sorry about Widget."

"Thanks."

Later that night in bed, I stared up at the ceiling, and wondered if I never left if Widget would still be alive. I missed my scraggly old cat. I guess his nine lives were up. I also missed the Thanksgiving dinners, and the family fighting about almost everything and nothing. Alcohol flowed freely at Grandma's, and everyone needed to be heard, and the drink gave them the courage to speak their minds. I rolled over and thought about what JD said about my mom being jealous of me. Why would she be jealous of me? What did I have that she didn't? I was sure this couldn't be true. Maybe this was what it meant when someone said you were too close to see. I closed my eyes and tried to remember what Widget looked like. A tear rolled down my cheek and a smile crossed my lips, thinking about him with a chicken leg in his mouth running down the street.

TWELVE

Capricorns stick to family traditions

On Christmas Eve, my dad would pick my sister and me up and take us to our grandmas' house. My dad had four sisters and two brothers, and there were a lot of cousins. Our Christmas dinner consisted of cheeseburgers and French fries from the Tastee Freeze, a fast-food restaurant My Aunts ordered ahead and I went with my dad and Uncles to pick up our food.

After we ate, we went in the basement where one of the concrete walls was papered with a red and white brick make-believe fireplace. We sang Christmas Carols and waited for Santa to come. We listened for the sleigh bells with our eyes on the staircase. Santa would come down the stairs saying, "Ho, ho, ho!" And each of us kids took turns sitting on his lap. He'd reach into a black garbage bag and pull out a present with our name on it.

All the cousins scattered around the house to open their gifts. My favorite thing to do was sit in the living room and watch the color wheel turn in front of my grandma's artificial silver Christmas tree, changing it from green to red and then blue.

This year, there was no tree, artificial or real, no paper fireplace, and no family. But I had JD. My dad sent my Christmas money early, and I used every cent to buy JD a present. I didn't care if I got anything. I only wanted to be able to give JD something.

Mom was in her room. *I'll Be Home for Christmas* was playing on the radio, and I was sitting in the living room looking out at the empty ski slope, thinking about an old boyfriend and another friend who came barging through my front door last year carrying a snow-covered Christmas tree they stole from the orphanage down the block that sold trees. I would never forget that Christmas, or my two friends who wanted me to have a tree that year.

There was a knock at the door. I jumped up and ran to open it. JD was standing there with snow covering his jacket and hat. He stomped his boots outside, knocking the snow off, and came inside. "Where is your Christmas tree?"

"Ah, we don't have a tree this year," I said.

"Let's go downtown. I want to give you your gift there. All the trees are lit up, and I want you to experience Breckenridge at Christmastime."

"I have your gift, too, but it's too big to bring with us, so you will have to open it here." I shuffled down the hallway to my room.

"You didn't have to get me anything," JD yelled.

"Well, I did. Now, sit down on the couch." When I got back in the living room, I handed JD his gift. "Merry Christmas, JDog," I said.

JD tore into the paper and pulled it away. "What is this?"

"New floormats. They're for your Jeep."

JD held up the black rubber winter mats. Two for the front and two for the back. "I love them. How did you know I needed them?"

"For one, yours smell like dead animals, and two…"

"You can stop now." JD chuckled. "These are great. I guess you want me to put these in now?"

"It wouldn't hurt."

He stood and planted a kiss on my lips. "Let's go."

I grabbed my jacket off the chair and pulled my hat out of my sleeve. I yelled down the hallway toward Mom's room. "I'm leaving, I'm going downtown with JD. I'll be back later." I waited for her to respond, but she didn't.

"She didn't even answer you. Does she ever respond to you when you talk to her?" JD asked.

"Yeah, sometimes. Let's go, JD."

JD carried his new floormats under his arm. He removed the old mats and installed the new ones. He threw the old ones in the dumpster next to our apartment building. It smelled like a new car now.

After a short drive downtown, we parked and walked to the center of the town. The night sky glowed from all the lit-up trees. Snow crunched under our boots. The sound of Christmas carolers singing brought back memories of when I'd go caroling with my church group when I was young.

Children's laughter and "Merry Christmas" greetings echoed in the night from everyone we passed. This was like a movie, like something you could only dream about. JD took my elbow and pulled me toward one of the smaller, less-crowded trees. A soft smile crossed his lips. "Merry Christmas, Sandy," He handed me a gift-wrapped box the size of a ring box.

Oh, no, not his class ring again.

"Open it. Open it," JD said.

"JD..."

"Open it."

I pulled my gloves off and ripped the paper. With a deep breath, I slowly opened the lid. It was a ring. The brown and gold stone sat in a silver setting. Rivers of green glimmered in the Christmas tree lights when I held it up. "Oh, my god, JD. It's beautiful."

I saw him smiling. Tears came to my eyes. "You didn't have—"

He pressed one finger to my lips. "It's a tiger eye. They say a tiger eye is supposed to balance toxic emotions and have healing properties."

"Are you reading that from something?"

"No, I memorized it from the paper that came with it."

"I definitely need this, don't I?"

"Put it on, let's see if it fits," he said.

I slid it onto my finger.

JD held both my hands in his. "It's perfect," he said.

I hugged JD. "This was the best Christmas ever." This was what I had been dreaming about my whole life. Breckenridge at Christmas time was picture perfect. Of course, Breckenridge at any time of the year was beautiful. I was so glad I came out here. I never wanted to leave. I was home.

* * *

January 17th

The day before my eighteenth birthday, JD and I met Jason and Clarissa at the ski resort. The slopes were packed.

Everyone in Breckenridge was there, along with a few thousand tourists.

"You ready to go?" JD asked.

"Do I look ready?" I nervously smoothed my rented ski apparel. "Did I ever tell you I don't know how to ski?"

"Learning how to ski is not going to kill you," he said.

"How do you know? It's a big mountain. I'm pretty sure if you fell off it would mean death."

"I know a lot. So, don't worry, I'll teach you what you need to know so you don't fall off and die."

"Ugh, and I'm afraid of heights too."

"What? Why didn't you tell me this before we started dating?" He laughed.

"Not funny, JD. How do I look?" I pushed my braids out of the way and pulled the goggles over my eyes.

"Like you know how to ski," he said.

"Yeah, I do look pretty good, don't I?" I checked myself out in the rental shop mirror.

If only I knew what I was doing.

"Come on, let's go before the snow melts." JD tugged me out the door.

We snapped on our skis and slid over to the chairlift at the bunny hill. This didn't look like the bunny hills we had in Illinois —those would be anthills here.

"We'll start on the bunny hill, then we'll move on once you get the hang of it," JD said.

I nodded.

If I don't die first.

We spent a few minutes on the flats. JD showed me how to keep my skis parallel to coast in a straight line, and how pushing out the back of my skis slowed me down so I could come to a stop.

"Now, push slightly harder with one leg, and your skis will take you into a turn," JD encouraged.

I practiced a few more times.

"You're doing great. I think we're ready to hit the slopes!"

We slid over to the chair lift and waited in line.

"When you feel the chair hit the back of your legs, sit down, hang on, and don't look down. Watch how the people in front of us do it," JD said.

"Why are all the people in front of us three feet tall?" I asked.

"Because they're kids, and if they can do it, you can, too. Are you nervous?"

"No. Maybe." Lying, of course.

"You'll be fine. Show these kids you know what you're doing."

Somehow, I managed to get on the chairlift successfully, even with the suspended bench rocking back and forth. I inched my butt as far back on the seat as I could and held on for dear life.

"What if my skis fall off?" I asked, looking down.

"They won't fall off. Hey, hey, I told you not to look down," he scolded.

"I can't help it. I'm trying to figure out where the best place is to land when I fall off this thing."

"You're too much. You'll be fine. Now, watch what I do, and stop looking down." JD took my chin in his gloved hand. "Look up here at me."

White powder snow blanketed the mountains. I could barely see the tops of the evergreens poking through the snow in some places. This was heaven. The skiers floated down the trails in their brightly colored parkas, snow spraying behind them. They made skiing look so easy.

"When the chair gets to the top, don't hesitate getting off. Jump off quickly and move out of the way," JD said.

"Out of the way from what?"

"The chairlift. Don't let it hit you in the back of the head." He chuckled.

"What? Now I have to worry about getting hit by the chairlift?"

"Here, take my hand and follow me," he said patiently.

When we got to the top of the hill, I stared down the steep incline. I pressed my hand firmly on my stomach and tried to catch my breath. My lips started quivering.

"This doesn't look like a bunny hill, JD."

"It is, don't worry. Bend your knees, stay loose, and don't let your skis cross as you go down."

"Okay," I said, mechanically, still staring down the mountain. I closed my eyes and said a silent prayer.

God, I don't want to die, not today.

"Are you ready to go?" JD asked.

"Yeah, I guess." I took a deep breath and let it out. The air leaving my mouth became a cloud of white.

Why is skiing so complicated? I don't think skiing is for me.

"Good, don't be scared. If you fall, you fall. Don't worry. Get back up and keep going."

"Okay," I said.

"As you go down the hill you want to cross the slope side-to-side. If you start going too fast, push the tails of your skis out, which will slow you down, but don't let the tips cross," he said.

"Okay," I said, nodding, filing this all in the back of my head.

"Let's go," He dug his poles into the fresh snow, getting traction and moving down the hill.

"Where are you going?" I yelled out to him as he skied away from me.

"I'm moving over here, so you don't crash into me." He grinned. "Don't worry, I'm not going anywhere. I'll be right here watching you."

"Here goes nothing," I said, trembling.

I started out slow my skis snow-plowing across the hill. My heart raced. My whole body shook, and my knees started to hurt.

"Relax," JD yelled.

"Relax, my butt," I mumbled.

JD must have been hating this, having to babysit me, but I knew he wanted me to learn how to ski so I'd be able to go with him. I let up on my snow-plowing a little and started to pick up speed, making wide cuts back and forth.

"I think I'm doing pretty good right now," I yelled, slowing to a stop.

"Yeah, you got it. Keep moving." Out of the corner of my eye, I saw a flash of red and then black, something bumped my shoulder, then my ski.

"Oh, my god, what was that?" I yelled out. I turned to look, but my skis crossed, and I started to lose my balance. I tried to correct myself but wobbled to my left. I thrust out one of my ski poles to stop my fall but ended up jabbing it into my ribs as I went down.

Oh, my god, I'm going to die.

God, if you can hear me, I don't want to die today.

Remember when I used to go to church every Sunday?

I listened to you, so, can you please help me out today?

With the wind knocked out of me, I hit the snow, hard. To my horror, I started sliding headfirst down the hill. Some bunny hill this was. If I was lucky, maybe I'd end up all the way back at the lodge. I wheezed, trying to catch my breath as I slid. Snow sprayed everywhere. After what seemed like forever, I came to a sudden stop. I think I hit a rock or a tree. A blanket of snow covered me. I tried looking up, but the snow inside my goggles masked my view.

"I gotcha. I gotcha," JD said. "Are you hurt?"

"I don't know," I said, brushing the snow from my goggles. I lifted my head to see what I managed to do to myself. I was covered with snow. I felt like a snowman who was run over by a snowplow.

"What did I hit?" I asked.

"Nothing. I stopped you from sliding," JD said.

"What did I do wrong?"

"Nothing, it wasn't you. Some asshole went flying down the hill and knocked you down."

"I tried to do what you told me to do. I didn't know how to stop myself from falling."

"Don't worry about that. Can you stand?"

"I'm gonna sit for a minute. Where are my poles?" I asked.

"Ah, back there," he said, pointing up the hill.

I sat up and looked back up the hill. My poles were laying in the snow.

How the hell am I going to get those? I wonder if I could leave them there.

I slowly stood up. I felt a burning pain in my ribs. I bent over, holding a mitted hand on my rib cage.

Don't cry. Don't cry.

"What's wrong? Why are you holding your ribs?"

"I think I broke my ribs, my legs, my back and maybe my butt—"

"I doubt you broke everything, but you did have a nasty fall. Sit down and don't move. I'm going to go back up the hill to get your poles," he said.

"Oh, don't you worry, I'm not going anywhere." And then I noticed I only had one ski. "JD, while you're up there, look for my ski, too."

JD sidestepped up the hill.

I waited for him to get back with my gear. I didn't think he'd ever ask me to go skiing with him again. Why did I agree to come here today?

"Here's your ski and poles. Hold onto my arm and stand up. Use your pole to steady yourself and stick your boot back in the binding," he said.

"It's not going in. Is it broken?" God, please don't let this ski be broken. My mom would kill me if I had to pay for a new ski.

JD bent down to study the ski and my ski binding. "No, it isn't broken. Put your boot in toe first, then push the heel down hard."

"It's not working." Tears started to roll down my frozen cheeks.

"Hey, why are you crying?"

"I don't know. I feel like I'm ruining your day. I—"

"Stop. You're not ruining my day. I know you didn't know how to ski. It's my fault for pushing you to come. And it's not your fault that jerk hit you. He shouldn't even be on this hill."

Yeah, he shouldn't have been here on this hill, and neither should I.

"JD, I wanted to try—I want to be able to do the things you enjoy, but I suck at this. And this stupid boot won't go in."

"You don't suck. You need more practice and maybe some lessons. Brush the snow off your boot and try again."

The boot clicked in.

"And, besides, we do lots of things together. Skiing doesn't have to be one of them. Now, stop crying, or your face will freeze."

"Thanks, JD. Thanks for being here for me," I said.

"I'll always be here for you. Let's ski down the rest of the way. We'll go slow, and I'll stay close."

My body heaved in relief. I fell. I failed, and JD was still there for me. JD saved me from death.

When we got down to the bottom of the hill, I collapsed onto the first bench I saw. "I'm staying here, I'm not moving."

"Take off your skis, and let's go inside and warm up," he said.

Okay. I'd move if it meant warming my frozen body.

I wobbled getting up. "Think I need a beer."

"I need more than a beer." He winked at me.

"What about Jason and Clarissa?"

"I'll meet up with them after I get you inside," he said.

My knees wobbled as I walked over to a massive fireplace in my ski boots. I spied a chair where I was going to sit for the rest of the afternoon. I unzipped my jacket, shook out the snow, and slid it off, letting it drop to the floor.

"I'm going to hang out here until you're done," I said, melting into the overstuffed chair.

"Are you sure?" JD asked.

"Yeah, I'm sure. I'm sorry. I wish I was better at skiing."

"You can't be great at everything."

"Yeah, but I want to be great at everything. I don't want to be a failure."

Nobody likes a failure.

"You're not a failure. You try too hard, and you don't need to. And I don't like you any less because you couldn't ski." He kissed my cold lips.

"Do you want me to get you anything before I go back out?"

"No, I'm fine. Go find Jason and Clarissa," I said.

"Try and relax. I'll see you later." He went back into the cold. Snow started falling, and I was glad I had a nice warm spot to forget my attempt at skiing and death.

After warming up, I got up to walk, but the pain in my calves stopped me. I unclipped my boots and pried them off. Ah, my legs were free. I shuffled over to the beverage counter and ordered a hot chocolate, paying with a crumpled ten-dollar bill I had stuffed in my bra.

When I got back to my seat, I reclined into my chair. I thought about my skiing debacle with JD. He always did everything right all the time and I couldn't even get my boot into my binding. And those stupid skis, why were they so long? Maybe I did need lessons, not only in skiing, but in life, too.

Off in another room, piano music started playing. I turned to see where it was coming from. My mom never played the piano much, but I used to love to listen to her when she did. I could have listened to her making music forever. She was a different person when she played. She was beautiful. Every time I heard the piano, I thought of those days a long time ago when I thought she loved me.

A man wearing black pants and a white-button down shirt with a red tie walked over to me. "Can I get you anything?" He asked.

"No. I'm okay. But do you know what song the piano player is playing?" I asked.

"The name of the song is Clair de Lune."

"Thank you."

A few years ago, my mother sold our piano. I was never told why.

A lump rose in my throat as I thought about her. I pushed back the tears that wanted out, but one escaped and dropped into my hot chocolate. The tear drop swirled around, spreading across the dark liquid-heaven and then disappeared. I let another one fall and watched it do the same.

An hour or so later, JD, Jason, and Clarissa were back from skiing. They found me in the lounge, relaxing by the fireplace.

"Hey, Crash, how you feeling?" Jason asked, gripping my knees.

"Oh, you mean me, Jason?"

"Yeah, you. I heard you made a mess on the hill out there."

"Very funny. I'm still alive, just trying to rest my broken body."

"I'm glad you didn't get hurt. That's all that matters. But I wish I could have seen it," Jason said, sitting on the couch across from me with Clarissa.

"Yeah, thanks. And I'm glad you weren't there to see it," I said.

"You look comfortable," JD said, sliding into the chair next to me. "What are you drinking?"

I passed my cup to JD. "Hot chocolate, but it's not hot anymore." He took a few sips, tear drops and all.

Jason tapped Clarissa's knee. "Ready to go?"

"Yeah, I'm ready," she said.

"JD, we gotta run," Jason said getting up from the couch.

"Yeah, alright. Great skiing today, Jason."

JD and Jason fist-bumped. "Yeah, it was fun. And JD, I'll beat you down the run next time."

Jason nudged my arm. "See ya, girl."

Clarissa offered a hug. "Hey, at least you tried. You'll get the hang of it."

Not in this lifetime.

"Yeah, thanks, guys. See you later," I said.

After they left, JD stroked my arm. "What do you want to do now?"

"I was thinking, I'd get my skis back on and ski down that double black diamond run and see if I can break the rest of my body."

"I'd say let's go, but it's dark, and the mountain is closed."

"Oh, darn." I laughed. "Did you have fun today?"

"Yeah, I did. I wish you would have had fun, though," JD said.

"I'm good. What do you think about getting a hotel room for the night?"

"I don't have that kind of cash on me," he said.

"How much are the rooms here?" I asked.

"Ah, like four hundred a night."

"Are you kidding me?"

"No, this place is not cheap. And I can't put it on my credit card, either. My dad would see the charge and freak out. Let's go back to your place and order a pizza, and I'll massage your broken body." He slid his hand down my back. "I'll start with your butt," he said.

"Oh, I could go for a massage. Now you're talking."

"You think your mom will be home?" JD asked.

"Are you kidding? She's never home."

"How do you do it?"

"Do what?"

JD swept me up in his arms. "Pretend like it doesn't hurt when your mom does this shit to you?"

I tilted my head back. My eyes met his. "It's not like she's beating me."

"It's still abuse, and wrong," he said in a firm voice.

I nodded my head slightly. "JD…"

"I know, you don't want to talk about it." He pulled me to my feet. "Let's go."

THIRTEEN

Capricorns like life in black and white

"I like this ring on you," JD said.

He held my hand up in the moonlight shining through my bedroom window. "It's so pretty next to your green eyes. Do you like it?"

"Yeah, I do like it. I told you that when you gave it to me on Christmas."

"You did, but I want to make sure you really like it."

"Yes, I really...like it," I said.

"Good, I have something else for you."

"What?"

He picked his jeans up off the floor and slid his hand into one pocket. JD held a wrapped box in front of me.

I sat up next to him.

"Happy Birthday," he said.

"You remembered?"

"Of course I did. Oh, wait, your birthday is tomorrow, isn't it?"

I took the box from him. "Yeah, but you can still give me my gift today."

"What did you say it was your...?"

"Golden birthday. I'm eighteen on the eighteenth." I shook the box. "What is it?"

"Quit shaking it and open it."

I tore into the paper, revealing a black velvet box.

"It's a tiger eye. Oh, JD, it's so pretty." I pulled the necklace away from the prongs holding it in place.

"It matches your ring."

I held the necklace beside my ring. "I love it. This tiger eye has more green flecks in it."

"Yep, that's why I got it. It matches your eyes."

"Help me put it on."

JD clasped the necklace around my neck. "I wanted you to have something special for your birthday." He laid down and rolled onto his side.

"I do… You're here with me right now," I said.

"What did you get from your mom?" JD asked.

"Nothing yet. She's taking me out for dinner tomorrow night. I got a card from my dad and stepmother yesterday—and, of course, nothing from my sister, as usual."

"When will your mom be home tonight?"

"I don't know. My mom comes and goes. I never know. Did I tell you she's going out with this guy she met at work?"

"No, I don't think you did. That was quick. Have you met him yet?"

"Yeah, only once. He seems nice, but my mom's been acting weird lately. I think she might be up to something."

JD stroked my arm, making circles with his finger.

A shiver ran through my body as I remembered my mother stroking my arm when I was little. Many years ago, she had stopped and now JD was taking her place. My heart was full again.

"You know, you're so easy to talk to," he said.

"What do you mean?"

"I feel safe talking to you, like I can tell you anything," he said rolling onto his back. "And, no matter what I tell you, I never have to worry you'll judge me."

I took his chin and turned his face toward mine. "Why would I judge you? I mean, look at all the things I told you about my mom, and you've never judged me, have you?"

"No, but I don't need anyone who is perfect."

"What?"

"I mean, I'm not perfect, so, I guess what I'm trying to say is, I don't want everything to be perfect. Ah, my arm is falling asleep." He shifted and pulled his arm out from underneath me.

"What do you mean? You're great at everything," I said.

"That's the problem. I have to be great at everything I do. I have to be the perfect son, throw the perfect touchdown pass, score the most points in basketball, and strike everyone out in baseball. Everyone expects me to be a superstar athlete. Sometimes I wished my arm would break, and then I'd have an excuse to not have to be perfect anymore."

"I think I'd rather be a superstar athlete than be hidden in your own life. I used to dream about getting sick or have some disease, so my mom would stay home and take care of me, telling me she could never live without me. And then I found that tumor, but it didn't change anything." I caught my breath.

She told me over, and over that I was crazy, that there was nothing there.

I begged her to take me to a doctor. I wanted the doctor to tell me I was crazy.

He didn't tell me I was crazy. I was not crazy.

I am not crazy.

JD caressed my scar. "You're not hidden, and you will always be right here beside me... forever."

I rolled over on my back and stared at the ceiling. "When I moved out here, all I wanted was to find someone to love me and care about me."

"You know I love you, don't you?"

I caught myself before I laughed, because I saw the seriousness in his face. I rested my head on his chest. I couldn't look at him right now. I wanted to cry, but I wasn't sure if I should or not. Oh, my god, this was what I'd been waiting for my whole life, someone to tell me they loved me, and I didn't know how to act. A tear escaped and ran down my cheek. I knew he could feel it when it landed on his chest. I held him tighter.

January 25th.

A week after my birthday, I came home from school to find Mom in her bedroom. My heart sank when I saw her packing a suitcase. Oh, my god, this was why she was acting so strange lately.

"What's up?" I asked, standing in her doorway.

Her voice empty of emotion she said, "I'm moving back home."

"What? You've got to be kidding me." My voice shook slightly. "Why?"

I couldn't believe this was happening again. A single tear ran down my cheek, then more flooded my face. I had no problem crying in front of her now, but I refused to sob. I wanted her to see how much this was hurting me. She'd probably think I'm weak and I'd go home with her. The tears

I wiped away were black from my mascara. My mother was ruining everything.

I rushed over to her in an attempt to make her look at me. Her eyes were cold as ice.

"Mom, will you please tell me what's going on?"

She continued to pack.

"If you think for one minute, I'm leaving with you this time, you're crazy!" I cradled my head in my hands. It didn't stop the pounding at the thought of having to leave the life I'd carved out here—school, my friends, JD. "Don't you understand I graduate in five months? What is wrong with you…? I'm not going. I'm not going anywhere with you!"

My arms and legs trembled as I stormed to my room. Nausea filled my stomach.

God, please make it stop, please make it stop.

Before I got to my room, my mother yelled down the hall. "I'm leaving in the morning, with or without you."

"Fine, go ahead and leave."

"The rent for this month has been paid, so you can stay here until then. After that, you're on your own."

I slammed the door and sank to the floor. I wished I could have fit in my closet and hid from her. My breath caught sharply in my throat. My chest was empty after having my heart ripped out. I didn't care anymore that she was leaving. She didn't care about me or my life, not here or anywhere. I wasn't running away with her again. Moms weren't supposed to run away. These last five months I realized crying didn't make me weak, it meant I could care and love. I held my tiger eye necklace in my hand, knowing JD loved me.

* * *

The next morning, JD picked me up for school. He could tell I'd been crying. He asked me what was wrong, but I shook my head and said it was nothing, and we'd talk later.

After school, He pulled into the Supersaver parking lot and put his Jeep in park.

"Now you're going to tell me what happened, and I'm not taking you home until you do," he said.

I stared out the window, and then down at JD's floor mats, remembering our Christmas together.

"Start talking," he demanded.

"Oh, my god… She's doing it again."

"Who? What are you talking about?"

"She's leaving…"

"Your mom?" He yelled.

I nodded.

JD banged his fist on the dashboard. "She can't do that," he said.

"She's done it before."

He let out a breath and turned toward his side window.

Tears formed in my eyes. "JD, I'm not leaving, I'-mmm stay-ing here. I don't know what I'm going to do, but I'm not going with her."

He pulled back onto the road and drove to my apartment. We pulled into the parking lot. My mother's car was still in her parking space. The door to our apartment opened. My heart pounded as she came down the stairs with her suitcases. I got out of JD's jeep and walked to her.

"For the last time, I'm leaving," she said. "You still have time to pack and come with me."

"I already told you, I'm not going." JD was still in his Jeep. I didn't want him to get involved, not now. "How can you just leave me?"

"I'm not leaving you. You are leaving me by not coming." She put her suitcases inside the car. "You can still come home with me."

I straighten my back and brushed my tears away. "I am home," I said. I didn't want her to leave. I wanted her to stay. I wanted to be able to show her what a good daughter I was. I needed her to tell me she loved me, just once. "Why are you doing this?" I asked.

"I want what you have—someone to love me," she finally said.

I had to step back when she closed the car door. She backed out of her parking spot and drove away. I ran toward her car. "But I do love you…Mom," I yelled.

She turned the corner, and she was gone. My knees buckled underneath me. JD ran toward me, lifting me up before I hit the ground.

"JD, I can't…I -I can't breathe." I started sobbing.

He lifted me and pulled me into him. "I got you. I got you."

"JD, please don't leave me. Please don't ever stop loving me."

"I'm not going anywhere, and I'm never going to leave you," he said.

"I don't know how I'm going to do this alone," I said.

"I don't know how either. I'll talk to my dad tonight. You should go talk to your guidance counselor tomorrow and see what she thinks you should do."

JD helped me to my apartment.

"I want to be alone right now, JD."

"Are you sure?"

"Yes."

"I'll call you later."

I went into my room and laid down. I thought if I could sleep, then I'd wake up and this would all be a bad dream. I watched the afternoon sunlight shining on the walls fade to black from underneath my blanket.

My phone rang. I didn't want to answer it. I didn't want to talk to anyone, but maybe it was my mom calling telling me she was coming back. I picked up the receiver.

"How are you doing?" JD asked.

"I'm okay, I guess." I pulled the blanket off my head. "I'm so flipping mad right now. I fucking hate her."

"Yeah, so do I. She's gone now, so don't worry about her anymore. By the way, I talked to my dad about your mom leaving. He said since you're eighteen, you should be able to stay. The only problem is you need money. Do you think your dad will send you your child support if you could find someone to stay with?"

I sat up. "I didn't think about that."

"Can you call him and ask?"

"Yeah, I'll talk to him this weekend," I said.

"I can come over when you call him."

"No, I'll be okay."

I'll be Okay.

I fell back on my bed.

"You know, Sandy, you say you're okay all the time and saying 'it's okay' or 'I'll be okay' doesn't make everything okay," JD said.

"I say I'm okay, because I want everything to be okay. I don't want to think about all the bad things that have happened to me, so I say it's okay hoping it will be okay. I know it doesn't make sense to you, but it does to me. It's just what I do."

"All right, then. And you're right. Maybe everything will be okay. Try and get some sleep. I'll see you in the morning."

"I will. I wish you were here with me tonight. Good night, JDog."

"Me, too."

I hung up the phone, pulled the blanket back over my head, and called Holly.

"Hey… Holly."

"Uh oh, hey girl, you sound muffled. What's wrong?" Holly asked.

"I'm under my blanket." I was silent for a minute. "My mom left…again."

"What? Where is she going?"

"Home," I said.

"So, you're coming back?"

"No, I'm not coming back. I'm staying here, and right now I don't want to be with her either."

"What are you going to do?"

"I'm going to go talk to my counselor tomorrow and see what I have to do to stay here."

"Why don't you come back? You can stay with me."

"I know, but I want to finish school here, and I can't keep running away like she does all the time. Also, I can't leave JD."

"You shouldn't wrap your life up in one guy. I miss you," she said.

"I know… I miss you too."

Our apartment was always a little empty because Mom was rarely home, but now I was really alone. In the bathroom mirror, I tried to see the brave girl I really wanted to be. All my flaws and imperfections reflected back. I didn't see anything I hadn't seen before. I was still the same girl: the girl who tried everything to get her mother's love and attention. Was I not pretty enough or smart enough? Why couldn't she see me—the daughter she gave birth to, the daughter who looked like her? Could this be the reason Dad said there's no room for me in his house? Because he saw my mom in me and I reminded him of her and his failed marriage and his failures when he saw me?

Did my mom see me as a failure, too? Was that why she couldn't love me?

When I was younger, I'd sit on the sink in our bathroom and look in the mirror. I'd put my mother's makeup on to try and change the image I saw. No matter how much makeup I put on, I never changed. I was still the same, but with a lot more makeup. I held a warm washcloth over my face and cried. The mirror didn't lie— we lied to ourselves.

I didn't want to be the face behind my mother's makeup anymore.

Over the years, the mirror became my friend.

After a few minutes, I climbed into bed. Tomorrow was another day. I'd be okay.

FOURTEEN

Capricorns love being at home

When I got to school the next day, I didn't feel the same. I was different. I was not the girl I was back in September or before we came to Breckenridge, or who I saw in the mirror last night. Time changed me. People changed me, and birth control pills changed me, too.

I checked into the counseling office and asked to see my counselor, Karen Bartlett. I sat in a chair outside her office and waited a few minutes, which seemed like hours. I stared at the floor and hoped nobody would see me and wonder what I was doing there.

Karen's door opened.

"Come on in, Sandy," she said.

As soon as I was inside, I broke down and cried. She closed her door behind me. I told Karen everything, starting with why we came out to Breckenridge and what happened yesterday with Mom. I even told her about growing up without my mother on the weekends, what she did and what she didn't do, and I told her about *him*.

Karen gave me all the space and time I needed. She listened. She didn't say a word. By the time I finished, I drained myself of my old life. I finally told someone everything, and in the end, I was okay. The only damage was dried tears on my face.

"Karen, are there any foster families I can go to until school is out?" I asked.

Karen raised her eyebrows and sat back in her chair. "I've never had anyone ask me to find them a foster home before. You're eighteen, right?"

"Yeah, my birthday was two weeks ago," I said.

"So, you are considered an adult and you won't qualify for a foster home. We will need to find a way to work this out. I'll talk to whomever I need to make sure you can stay here until you graduate."

"How long will that take? I have to leave my apartment next week."

"I don't know, but I will work on this right away. Will you be alright on your own for a few days until we figure this out?"

"Yes, I'll be okay. I'm used to being alone."

Karen cleared her throat and blinked a few times. I knew what she was doing, because I used to blink back my tears too.

"Good, now wipe your tears and fix your mascara. Let's not worry about this anymore today. I'll get back to you in a day or two." She rested her hand on my shoulder. "If you want you can stay here until your next class."

"I'm okay. I'll go fix my makeup in the bathroom," I said.

After I left Karen's office, I heard her making a call on her speakerphone. My heart pounded as I leaned against the wall outside her office. I knew I shouldn't eavesdrop, but I wanted to find out who she was calling.

"Hey, Dan, got a minute?" Karen said.

"I've always got time for the hottest wife in town," I heard Dan say.

I rolled my eyes.

"I was just chatting with Sandy Kelly."

"Yeah, what's up? Don't tell me she's not going to play tennis for me this spring."

"No, but her mother went back to Chicago and left her here," she said.

"What? You're kidding."

"I wish I was. I guess her mother did this before," Karen said.

"Why didn't she go with her?" Dan asked.

"She said she didn't want to be uprooted again."

"So, now what is she going to do?"

"She doesn't want to leave, she wants to stay here. But she can't live on her own, she has one week to find a place to live. Dan, how would you feel about her moving in with us just until she graduates? Kelsey would like having an older girl around the house."

"What are your plans, and how is this going to work, Karen? We have an extra bedroom, but we can't support her financially," Dan said.

"I know. Dan, we have to find a way to help her. Sandy's been through so much, and you'll never believe what Sandy found in her mom's closet. I'll tell you about it tonight. I'll ask Sandy to talk to her father and see if he can send money to her. Then she'd have whatever she needed, a roof over her head and spending money."

"That could work. But that's a lot of ifs, Karen," Dan said.

"I'll call Sandy down after school and tell her what we're thinking. I'm sure she will be fine knowing she has a place to live and she won't have to leave," Karen said.

"Karen, don't get too excited. We still need to work out the details. And you should let Mrs. Adams know what we're thinking. I don't want any problems for her or us," Dan said.

I tuned out the rest of their conversation, and closed my eyes. I said a silent prayer this would work out. I'd asked a lot of stupid, trivial prayers, like asking God to make my boobs bigger and my butt smaller, but those prayers weren't answered. I was praying this one would be answered. This was a *real* prayer, God.

I snuck away from Karen's office. I was relieved to hear Karen and Dan wanted me to live with them.

Later that day, Mrs. Adams called me down to the office and told me what the Bartlett's were planning. God was listening.

Arriving home to my apartment after school, I realized this wasn't my home any longer. I went into the bathroom and found my mirror. I was growing up so fast. I looked past my reflection, not sure I recognized myself. I searched for the confidence I needed to call my dad and ask him for money.

What if he said no? If he did, I would f-n flip.

I took a deep breath, here goes nothing.

I picked up the phone and dialed his number.

Ring…ring…ring…ring…

"Hello?"

"Hi, Ellen," It figured. I built up all that courage, and my dad didn't even answer. "Can I talk to my dad?" I closed my eyes and waited for her to answer.

"Oh, Sandy… How are you?" She asked.

"I'm fine, I guess. Is Dad there?"

"I'm sorry, Sandy, your dad is in no condition to talk now… You know, he's been drinking. Can you call back tomorrow morning?"

This was not the first time I'd heard this. "Ah, yeah. I'll call back tomorrow," I said.

I worked up my courage for this?

"Make sure you call early," she finished.

"Yeah, I will. Goodbye, Ellen."

Saturday morning, without consulting my mirror, I picked up the phone again and dialed the ten digits I did yesterday.

"Hello?"

"Hey, Dad." He sounded tired or maybe hungover. "Uhm, Mom left and moved back home, and I need help." It was nice to hear his voice. I hadn't heard it in a long time. I wondered if he missed me at all?

"Jesus, what happened? Why did she leave? And where are you?" Dad asked.

"I'm still here in Breckenridge, and I don't know why she left. She never tells me anything. Uhm, Dad? Are you still there? Well, if you are, I have a place to live until I graduate in June. Mrs. Bartlett, my school counselor, and her husband, are willing to let me stay with them… So, I was wondering if you could send the child support check to me instead of Mom since she's no longer supporting me." I closed my eyes, heart pounding.

There was silence on the other end. "Give her what she needs." I heard my dad say in the background and then Ellen was on the phone.

"What's going on?" Ellen asked.

I should have just told her yesterday.

I repeated my story. It was much easier talking to her.

"I'm so sorry this is happening, Sandy. I wish there was more room for you, but your dad… we can't right now," Ellen said.

"Yeah, I know."

Maybe when I'm thirty.

"What's your address? I'll send you a check."

I gave her my new address, and she said, "I'll put it in the mail today, and I'll add a little extra to help you out, too."

"Thank you, Ellen. I love you."

"Aw, Sandy, I love you too, and so does your dad," she said.

Yeah, okay.

* * *

Everything worked out. Karen and Dan helped me pack and move in to their house two months ago. Their home didn't feel like a home to me yet. I told myself I'd only be here for three more months, and then I'd be gone. More than ever, I didn't know what I was going to do after I graduated. It was time to start thinking about my future.

Maybe I should join the military. Their motto was "Be all you can be."

And I wanted to be someone.

Spring Break started this weekend. JD and most of my friends would be gone for the week. Most of the locals left town on break to warmer climates. Out of towners flooded the ski resorts because the snow stayed until the end of April sometimes. Even though there was snow on the mountains, the sun was warm enough for people to ski without hats and Jackets, and some skied in shorts and tee shirts. Not me. I stayed off the slopes. My skiing days were over. This year, I would be shoveling snow and hanging out with the Bartlett's, and I was okay with this.

My family didn't go on vacation. But my Dad and his new family did. They went to Disney World every year. My sister and I weren't invited. It was like Dad forgot we were part of his family, too. When I'd visit them, it hurt to see the pictures of *their* vacations in the many photo albums displayed in their house.

It was late, and I hadn't heard from JD, which was odd, because we talked every night before bed. I called him from my room.

"Where were you after school?" I asked when he answered.

"Ah, I had a meeting with Coach Thomas," JD said.

"Oh, I was wondering why I couldn't find you. Is everything okay? You seemed kind of distant this morning," I said.

"Yeah, uhm, … We need to talk," he said.

"What do we need to talk about?"

"I think…how do I say this? We should break up while I'm in Cabo," JD said.

His words punched me in the gut. "What? What do you mean? Why?"

"I think I need some space," he mumbled.

I curled in on myself, knees pulled into my chest. "What does that mean? You need your space?"

"I need…some time to myself right now. I need to be alone for a while," he stuttered.

I jumped off my bed and started pacing. "You're joking, right?"

"No, I'm not," he said, forcefully but quietly. "It's just the way it's supposed to be."

"Why are you telling me this over the phone? Come over here and say this to my face."

"I can't...I..."

I felt the blood drain from my face. "JD, what's going on? Did I do something to make you feel this way?"

"No, it's not you— it's me. I need...some space right now." Now *he* sounded annoyed.

"Fine then," I yelled. "If this is what you want, I guess I don't have anything else to say. Goodbye, JD," I shouted.

"Wait—" he said,

I slammed the phone down and slumped down on my bed. "What the hell?" I couldn't believe JD broke up with me. He told me he loved me. What did he mean he needed his space? Space for what? I got up, staggered into my bathroom, and stood in front of the mirror. "Why does this keep happening to me? Why does everyone leave me?" My eyes watered. I dried them quickly. Crying wasn't going to help. I couldn't show weakness. I stood in front of the mirror, and told myself it would be okay... everything would be okay. I would be okay. Tomorrow was another day.

I washed my face and went back into my room. Before I turned out the light, I noticed the birth control pills on my nightstand.

Fucking pills.

This was all your fault. You changed me. It's your fault I fell in love with JD.

I'm done with you, too.

I threw them in the wastebasket next to my bed. They fell to the bottom through the paper and Kleenex. I pulled the covers over my head and closed my eyes. I fell asleep to the sound of rain falling on the roof.

The next morning, I trudged into the kitchen. Karen and Dan were eating breakfast, and Kelsey was running around, pushing her baby dolls in their stroller.

"You went to bed early last night," Karen said.

"Yeah, I was tired."

Karen and Dan looked at each other.

"Who were you yelling at on the phone last night?" Dan asked.

I held my hand over my stomach, watching Kelsey jabbering at her baby dolls. "Uhm…"

"Sandy, what's wrong, what happened?" Karen asked.

I listlessly put bread in the toaster. "JD broke up with me last night."

"He broke up with you the day before he left on vacation? Why would he do that?" Karen asked.

We both looked at Dan. He turned away.

"What did he say?" Karen asked.

"I don't know. All he said was he needed his space. Whatever that means."

Dan squirmed in his chair.

"Dan? Dan, you're a guy… Why would JD do this? Why would he break up with her right before vacation?" Karen asked, baffled.

Dan cleared his throat and pushed his cereal bowl to the side of the table. "Well, sometimes before guys go on vacation, they break up with their girlfriends so—"

"So, what, Dan?" Karen jumped in.

"So, in case they meet someone else— they can fool around," Dan said.

"What would be the point?" Karen demanded.

"So, they don't feel guilty about cheating. And when they get back home, the guys tell their girlfriends how much they really missed them and want them back."

Dan's words caught in my chest, making it hard to breathe. "What? Do you think that's what he wanted to do?" I asked, looking at them both.

"I don't know for sure, and certainly not from personal experience." Dan said, looking at Karen. "But I've known guys who have done this."

"Really? Like who?" Karen asked sharply.

"We don't need to get into this right now. We're talking about JD," Dan reminded her.

"So, is there a guidebook for guys telling them how to do this?" Karen asked.

"If there is, I never got one," Dan said.

"Well, if this is what JD wants to do, then fine with me. But if he thinks he can do this to me and then come home and try and get me back, he's has another thing coming," I said, boldly.

Karen smiled. "You go, girl. Don't let him treat you this way and get away with it. Also, Sandy, sometimes the best revenge is to date their worst enemy," Karen suggested.

"Don't tell her to do that, Karen," Dan scolded

"I'm not telling her to do it, but…"

"Thanks, guys, I'll figure this out. He's not going to get away with this. Thanks for having my back, Karen, and thanks, Dan, for telling me the truth about this. I've never heard about this player move before."

My toast popped up. I layered butter, sugar, and cinnamon on it and headed back to my room to start plotting my revenge.

FIFTEEN

Capricorns are very sensitive

In most of my relationships with friends and boyfriends, I found myself building them up. I've chosen to build people up rather than tear them down. I tried to show them how special they were and how to change things they didn't like about themselves. Somehow, though, I couldn't seem to find a way to build myself up the same way.

It really hurt that JD lied to me. He told me he loved me. He said he would never leave me. I guess I was wrong about him. I never should have trusted him. He was a dog. After I showered, I opened my closet door and decided I had nothing to wear. "Hey, Karen, do you want to go shopping with me? I've got nothing to wear," I yelled down the hall.

She appeared in my doorway. "A little retail therapy, huh?" She asked.

"Yep. I guess, do you want to go with me?"

"Yeah, let me get Kelsey ready, and we'll go," she said.

We drove to the mall downtown to begin my retail therapy session. I didn't know what it was about shopping that made me feel better. Was it making decisions on what to buy? Was it a feeling of accomplishment in finding the perfect shirt, dress, or boots? Or was it the pride that came with being a smart shopper and saving money with the buy one get one deals? Maybe it was as simple as looking into the mirror and seeing the change caused by that awesome blue shirt that would make any guy melt.

I voted for the last one.

"You know, I've never gone shopping with my mother," I said, sliding the hangered shirts back and forth on the rack.

"Why?" Karen asked.

"I don't know. She never wanted to go anywhere with me, and she was never home anyway. Even if she was home and I asked if she wanted to go shopping, she'd always say, 'Why would I want to do that?' I envied my girlfriends who spent the day shopping and getting manicures and having lunches with their moms." I stepped over to the next rack of clothes.

"I know it's not the same, but I hope you enjoy shopping with me and Kelsey."

"Oh, I do. This is nice. Maybe someday I'll have a daughter and go shopping with her. Yeah, maybe someday…And if I ever have a daughter, I'm going to name her Katniss."

"Katniss from *The Hunger Games*?" Karen asked.

"Yep, I want to be like her. I researched what Katniss meant. It's an edible plant, and there's a myth where Katniss's father tells her if she 'finds herself,' she'll never go hungry. When I have a daughter, that will be her name. I'll raise her to be an independent survivalist," I said.

"I'm sure you will," Karen said confidently.

"How about this shirt?" I asked, holding up a white tee with a green pot leaf on it.

"Ah, no, I don't think so. That's a marijuana leaf," Karen said.

"Ah, how do you know that, Karen?" I smiled at her.

A blush rose in her cheeks. "I've been around. I know a few things."

"Karen, why do you think my mom keeps leaving?"

"I don't know. I don't have an answer for that."

"Before she drove away, she said she wanted someone to love her. Why would she think I didn't love her?"

Karen didn't answer.

"And Why do you think JD left me?" I asked.

"Well, the last one is an easy one. JD's a jerk," Karen said.

We wandered into the shoe department. A pair of sparkling red shoes caught my

attention.

"Oh, Karen, check these out." I slipped them on. They were a little too big. "Do you think if I click my heals together, this would be like it never happened?"

"You mean coming to Breckenridge?"

"Ah, no. My life—my mom—everything."

"You know, Sandy, your mother may not be the mother you thought you should have… she's the mother you got."

Was it just that simple? You didn't get to choose your parents, and they didn't choose you either.

"But why do you think I kept going back to try and make our relationship work? And why do I miss her?"

"It's funny you should bring this up. Here, let's go sit over on that bench." We sat side by side. "There was a Dear Abby letter in today's paper. A woman who wrote her wanted to know why she yearned for her abusive mother after she grew up and moved away."

"What did Abby say?"

Karen rubbed her hands on her legs. "She said something like "Because the abuse I grew up with became a normal way of life for me." And later, when I finally found happiness and love, I thought something was wrong because I never had it. So, I found myself yearning for my mother, to feel normal. Any kind of abuse, whether it's physical, emotional or mental is, never normal." She took my hand in hers. "Please remember that."

Oh my god. Karen wrote that letter.

My mind raced back several years, thinking of all the things my mother did and said that were so hurtful and painful. "I don't want to hurt anymore, Karen. How do you make it stop?"

"By breaking the chain that has been holding you back. You have to free yourself from people who have hurt you." She hesitated for a minute.

Her words sunk inside me and run throughout my body. They were a part of me now.

Karen nudged my arm. "Let's go get a smoothie and toast to a new beginning," Karen said.

I followed Karen out of the store.

* * *

We sat outside, wearing our shades, enjoying our smoothies and the cool crisp air that was still hanging around from winter. The sun was high in the sky, bringing the warmth of spring.

I heard a voice. "Hi, Mrs. Bartlett, how are you?"

I peered over the top of my sunglasses at an awesome-looking guy standing near our table. It was Tom Carrillo. I'd seen him so many times, and now he was standing right in front of me. I brushed my fingers across my lips to make sure

I didn't have any smoothie juice on them and slid forward in my chair to make myself more noticeable.

"Hi, Tom. I'm good, how are you?" asked Karen.

He brushed a wave of blond hair off his forehead. "I'm good, too. No vacation this year?" Awesome guy—Tom—said. As he talked, he kept glancing over at me.

"No, we decided to stay home. How about you? What have you been up to?" Karen asked.

"I'm working full time at my parents' ranch, and I'm going to flight school to learn to fly helicopters," Tom answered.

"How nice. Good luck with that." Karen said. "Tom, have you met Sandy? She's staying with us until she graduates in June."

"We've sorta met a couple of times. It's nice to see you again, Sandy."

I gazed into his clear blue eyes. "Hi," I said sweetly.

"Aren't you going out with McCarron?" Tom asked.

Before I could answer, Karen jumped in. "No, she's not. She's single." She smiled.

I gave her a look.

Please stop. You're embarrassing me.

"Ah, that's nice to hear. Then, how would you like to go to the rodeo tomorrow?" Tom asked.

"Oh, that's right, your parents put on the rodeo every year, don't they?" Karen asked

"Yep, it starts tomorrow and ends Monday. How about it, Sandy? You can be my guest."

"Sure, I've never been to a rodeo before," I said.

"Really?" Tom asked.

"Nope, they didn't have rodeos in Chicago, but they have the Chicago Bulls," I said.

"Haha, nice… a girl with a sense of humor. Great, I'll pick you up at 10 am tomorrow?"

"Sure. Do you know where the Bartlett's live?"

"I sure do. I'll pick you up tomorrow, Sandy. Nice to see you, Karen," Tom said.

A smile flickered on my lips as he skipped down the stairs, hopped into his white pickup, and drove away.

"Oh, my god, Karen, he's gorgeous."

"Yes, he is. His parents own a ranch a few miles outside Breckenridge," Karen said.

"Yeah, I heard. How old is Tom?" I asked.

"Nineteen or twenty. He graduated two years ago. And, if I remember correctly, he and JD never got along," she added, smirking.

"Why not?"

"Tom went to school at Valley Christian, and he played football, basketball, and baseball like JD does. Even though JD is younger, the two of them have been competing for a long time. They're both good-looking guys, and I have a feeling they competed off the field too."

"With girls? JD dated Jessica for two years, so why would they have to compete?"

"JD and Jessica dated off and on. I think Tom may have had something to do with that."

So, Tom has been JD's competition.

"Oh, good to know," I said.

Karen threw our smoothie cups in the trash. "Let's go back inside the mall and get you something to wear tomorrow, cowgirl."

As promised, Tom picked me up promptly at ten o'clock. I was still in my room when the doorbell rang.

I pulled my best jeans on. They hugged me everywhere, making my butt look phenomenal, and I paired them with a tight white V-neck. I'd never dressed for a rodeo before, but I'm going to try to lasso myself a cowboy. I took one last look in the mirror to make sure I was perfect. I wasn't just perfect, I was hot.

When I bent down to tug on my new dark blue cowboy boots, my eye caught my birth control pills in the garbage can. I pulled them out and placed them back on my nightstand.

Okay, I'll give you one more chance.

Tom pulled up to the property housing the makeshift rodeo arena and grandstands. He parked his dusty white pickup in the back, behind the stands.

"Oh, my god, is this all yours? I mean, your family's?" I asked.

"Yep, this is all our land. Our ranch is down the street outside of town." He jumped out of the truck and placed a white cowboy hat on his head. Even with his hat on, Tom wasn't as tall as JD, but he was a perfect height for me.

"And this is where you work?" I asked, walking over to him.

"No. I don't work here. I work out at the ranch."

"Are you the boss?"

"Haha, no. I work for my parents, but when they retire, my brothers and I will take over and run this ranch and the one in Durango, which is twice the size of this one." He spread his arms out in front of him to encompass all the land and asked, "So, what do you think so far?"

"Uhm, I don't know… this place is so big."

"You need a cowboy hat, Sandy. Let's go find one," he said.

Tom took my hand, sending a tingle up my arm. His hands were rough and strong. There was a confidence in the way he wrapped his fingers between mine. We entered a tent with a white sign flapping in the wind that read, 'Carrillo's Western Wear.' He picked up a white hat with a brown band, identical to his, and placed it on my head. He brushed my hair out of the way. "This one should do." He stepped back. His teeth glimmered in a smile while he admired his work. "Perfect. I hope you like it."

I checked myself out in the mirror hanging from the frame of the tent. "It's perfect. Thanks, Tom," I said, sugar-sweet.

Oh, my god, what's gotten into me?

Do guys actually fall for this?

Tom nodded in the direction of a woman working in the tent. "Put this on my account." He extended his hand toward the exit. "Let's go find our seats. The rodeo is about to start."

"Don't we need to pay for the hat?" I asked.

"Nope, we own all the merchandise here, too, but you can pay me back later if you'd like." He winked.

"Sure, as long as you take stolen credit cards." I winked back.

Tom led me over to the grandstand, and we took our seats in the front row. The rodeo began with the crowning of Miss Breckenridge. Calf roping was next.

"What happens in the Calf roping." I asked.

"A Calf is let loose in the arena. A Cowboy on horseback charges out of the gate, chasing it while throwing a loop of rope from a lariat around the calves' neck. Then, he jumps off the horse and runs after the calf and ties its legs."

"How do they know who wins?"

"The Cowboy with the quickest time wins," Tom answered.

"So, the baby calf lays there with his legs tied squirming in the dirt?"

"Don't worry. The Rodeo clowns will untie it and shoo him out of the arena."

"Do they get hurt?"

"No, the Cowboys don't get hurt roping."

"I mean the calf."

Tom laughed a little and rubbed his hand along my thigh. "The calves will be fine."

Bareback Barrel racing was next, followed by cattle rustling.

"Now, the main event is bull riding. See the bulls lined up outside the gate?"

"Yep."

"These bulls can weigh up to eighteen hundred pounds. Coming out of the gate, the rider must stay on the bull for at least eight seconds, one hand holding onto the rope and the other in the air. Otherwise, he's out."

"Eight seconds? That doesn't sound very long."

"It is to a bull rider," he said, laughing.

"Have you ever ridden a bull?" I asked.

"Hell no, have you seen the size of those things? I like my body the way it is—in one piece," he said.

Yeah, so do I.

I found myself staring at his chest as it rose, straining against his shirt when he talked.

I wonder how big his heart is?

A blush covered my cheeks.

Getting off the subject of Tom's body, every guy here wore all the traditional cowboy gear - hats, tight jeans with big belt buckles, cowboy boots, spurs, beards, and long hair. And did I mention tight jeans? I'd concluded I really liked cowboys, and I may have been wrong about men in tight jeans.

After the rodeo, we drove to Tom's ranch. He pulled off the highway. Dust and gravel kicked up behind the truck as we approached a massive gate with a giant C, for Carrillo, on each of its double iron doors. He pressed a button on his visor, and the gates slowly opened. We drove down a long paved road that circled in front of a massive stone and log house.

"Here we are," he said, parking his pickup. "I hope you're hungry, because my dad has been grilling all day."

Tom opened my door for me.

I jumped out of his truck. "Yeah, I'm starved," I said.

When we entered the double doors, I slowed to a halt. Enormous wooden beams supported a cathedral ceiling. Floor-to-ceiling windows ran along the four walls, offering a breathtaking view of the pool and the vast land beyond. Lights twinkled in antler chandeliers hanging from exposed rafters. A fireplace big enough to drive a truck through took up the far wall.

"This is beautiful, Tom. I've never seen anything like it before."

"Come on, I'll show you the rest of the house after dinner," he said, leading me into the kitchen.

On the kitchen table was a spread of every type of grilled meat you could imagine. The scents of the meats and spices hung in the air. Colorful grilled vegetables snuggled together on platters, along with bowls of fresh-cut fruit.

The Carrillo's sure did know how to eat.

I asked Tom to point out the beef since I wasn't at all adventurous when it comes to meat.

After dinner, Tom gave me a tour of the house, and then took me out to the horse barn. We strolled along the immaculate pine floor, poking our heads in each stall.

"Oh, my god, Tom, they're beautiful. How many horses do you have?"

"Right now we have 25."

"I want to ride every one of them," I said.

"So, you like to ride?"

"I love to ride." I slid my hand through the iron bars and stroked the horse's velvety muzzle while gazing into his big brown eyes. "I love how horses have such free spirits and are so powerful, and so graceful. And I love how they let you take control of them, but still let you know they're in control too."

"This is Tony," Tom brushed his hand along Tony's mane. Tony bobbed his head as if nodding in approval.

"Is Tony your horse?" I asked.

"No, the black stallion at the end is mine," Tom said.

We found Tom's horse at the end of the stable.

"He's beautiful, Tom," I said.

Tom puffed out his chest and grinned, "Yes, he is."

"He looks so strong. What's his name?"

"Warrior. And yes, he's *very* strong and powerful." Tom opened the gate and stroked Warriors shiny black coat. "Where did you ride in Chicago?" He asked.

"My friends and I used to ride west of the city. They only let us walk them on trails, though. I wanted to run them. So, when we went riding, I'd take my horse to the back of the line and stop and wait until all the horses were ahead. Then, I'd run my horse to catch up. That's the only way I like to ride. You can't feel their power unless they're running. Have you ever seen wild horses and how they run free? They go where they want to go and they don't need anyone to guide them. Some days I wish I could be a horse and run free."

"I'm glad you like horses and that you want to be powerful, too. Somehow, I think you are already powerful. We'll take Tony and Warrior out for a run this week while you're off school."

"Yeah, I'd love that." Nobody had ever called me powerful before. I kinda liked it. Maybe I was, and I just didn't know it.

We strolled to the backyard. Small white lights were strung along the perimeter of the yard and patio. There was a custom pool with a ten-foot waterfall made of various-sized boulders and black lava rock at one end. There was a hot tub big enough to fit at least ten people at the other. We sat on a couple of lounge chairs overlooking the ranch.

"I know it's too cold to go in the pool, but how about jumping in the hot tub and relaxing a bit?"

"I'm sure it would feel great, but I'm going to pass tonight."

And every night. No more hot tubs for me. Stop thinking about JD.

"Do you know what time it is?"

Tom pushed his sleeve up. "It's 10:15."

"It's getting late. I should be getting home."

"You really have to leave so soon?"

"Yeah, I have a curfew," I said.

"All right, let's get you home. I don't want to get you in trouble," Tom said.

Tom pulled into Karen and Dan's driveway.

"Did you have a good time today?" he asked, turning to me.

"Yes, I did. Thanks for inviting me, and thanks for my new hat."

Tom lifted both our hats off our heads and kissed me. I hadn't kissed anyone other than JD in months. It was nice and different, too. We kissed for a while before he pulled away.

"I'd like to go out with you again if you're interested," Tom said.

I nodded and kissed him again. His lips broke away from mine and he started kissing my neck, pulling my shirt down over my shoulders. Unexpectedly he pulled back. "I've got to say good night."

I didn't want him to stop. There was something about a man's lips on my shoulders that drove me crazy. I pulled my shirt back up on my shoulder and caught my breath.

"Let's plan something for tomorrow night – How about dinner and then a horseback ride with Tony and Warrior?"

"Sounds good. I'd love to go riding, Tom." I open the truck door and jumped out.

"Oh, here… Don't forget your hat," he said, handing it to me through his open driver side window.

I put my hat on and tipped it toward him. "Thanks again, Tom. See you tomorrow."

"I'm taking you to a nice place for dinner tomorrow night, so wear something nice!" He yelled out the window.

"See you tomorrow," I said.

I climbed into bed. My head was swimming.

Oh, my god, he's so good-looking and such a good kisser, and most importantly, he didn't push me to do anything tonight.

I picked my pills up from the nightstand and popped one into my mouth.

Thank God I didn't stop taking these.

SIXTEEN

Capricorns are born to lead

The next night, Tom picked me up in a shiny red sports car—no pickup truck tonight. I wore a black dress and heels. My hair was pulled back in a soft ponytail, and I opted for lipstick instead of lip gloss. Tom wore nicely-fitted dress pants, a button-down shirt, and dress shoes. This was a significant change from yesterday and quite different from any date with JD.

"You look nice tonight," Tom said.

"You do, too," I said.

I could get used to this.

I wondered if any of my classmates had been to this restaurant, or if I was the only one. I was feeling special. I didn't feel like I was only eighteen. The waiter handed me a menu that could have passed for a finely bound leather book in a prestigious library. Tom must have really like me to bring me here and spend that kind of money on me. I was worth it, though. I needed to think about me and what made me happy. I remembered what Karen said about breaking the chain that held me down. I had to start—one link at a time. Unlike my mother, Tom saw *me* and who I was. I only had to be myself. I didn't have to try to be someone else. I didn't have to act out or prove I deserved to be treated better. Plus, he said I was powerful.

All the entrees were in French. I searched the menu for something that sounded like normal food. Pictures would have been better. I looked up at Tom, eyes wide.

"Order the Filet de Boeuf."

I slowly arched my eye brows.

"It's Filet Mignon," he said, smiling. "You'll want it cooked medium."

I mouthed a thank you. "What are you having?"

"The swordfish."

Ewe.

I'd been to nice restaurants with my grandparents for special occasions but never on a date. I wondered why Tom chose this place. Was he trying to impress me? Part of me was impressed, and part of me was nervous. But I did enjoy dressing up. When I was young, I would page through the Sears catalog at my grandmother's house. I'd spend hours looking at all the dresses. I circled the ones I wanted and made a wish list. I took the catalogue to my mother to show her, but, my wish for even one dress was ignored. Maybe she didn't want me to be prettier than her.

"After dinner, I have something planned for us when we get back to my house. I think you'll enjoy it." A smile flashed across his face.

My eyes widened. "What is it?"

"You'll see. Finish your Filet. But don't let me rush you."

The last time someone said they had a surprise for me I lost my virginity in a hot tub.

After Tom finished his swordfish and I finished my Filet Mignon, we drove back to his house. He poured two after-dinner drinks from a clear round bottle with the word "Port" written on the side and pushed a cork back inside.

"Here you go." Tom handed me a short round glass with dark red liquid in it. "Have you ever had port before?"

"No, I haven't."

"It's a sweet wine. My uncle makes his own wine." Tom swirled the port in his glass. I did the same. "Cheers." Tom tapped my glass.

We both raised our glasses to our lips.

"Yum, this is nice. It's sweet—and has a powerful kick to it. I think I like this."

He smiled and refilled my glass. "Yes, kind of like you." He kissed me softly on the lips, he took my hand, and we walked out to the patio.

So, now I've got a kick to me and I'm powerful.

Tom sat on one of the chaise lounges and pulled me down on top of him. I nestled myself between his legs. Above, stars danced through the sky while clouds surfed under them. A high-pitched howl echoed in the darkness, followed by a couple of barks.

"What's that noise? Is that an animal?" I asked.

"Those are coyotes. They howl to let the other pack members know where they are."

I shifted closer to him.

"Don't worry. They're far away," Tom said, with a slight laugh.

"They sound so close."

"Sound travels farther on a calm night." He wrapped his arms around my shoulders. "If they come any closer, I'll protect you."

The more I drank, the further I sank into Tom's body. My eyes closed for a moment, and I just enjoyed the warmth of the port and his body behind me. It was like being surrounded by a warm blanket.

"Hand me your glass," he whispered.

I opened my eyes and handed my glass to him. He set it on the table beside him. He wrapped his arms tighter around my body. I covered his arms with my own.

"When I'm around you, I can't think of anything else. I really enjoy being with you," Tom said.

I tilted my head to the side. Tom was smiling at me. He lowered the straps of my dress and his lips found my bare shoulders. He kissed them lightly--once, twice, three times. Warmth spread outwards from my heart to my fingertips and toes. I touched the side of his smooth-shaven face. I ran my fingers through his hair as his warm lips touched mine. He moved his hand from my waist and trailed his fingers down my arm, taking my hand in his.

"When you're ready, Sandy, I want to make you feel special," he said.

I didn't need to wait. I knew what I wanted, and that was him. I wanted Tom. His eyes bore into mine like he could see my soul. He was searching for an answer. He needed to hear the words that were stuck in my throat.

"I'm ready, Tom," I mouthed.

The corners of his mouth twitched before breaking into a grin. He kissed my forehead, the top of my nose, my chin, and then my lips. He slid out from beneath me, taking my hand in his, and pulled me to my feet. My heart knew what was coming. It beat rapidly. My skin warmed.

Inside, Tom led me through the dimly lit house until we approached an open door. A bed waited for us to one side. We crossed the threshold, and he turned the light on, closing the door with his foot.

"You're sure about this? I don't want you to feel pressured because I said…"

"Shh, this is where I want to be," I whispered.

He lowered the zipper of my dress. The fabric fell away from my body and caught on my hips. I tugged my dress the rest of the way and stepped out of it, leaving it to rest on the floor.

Tom stepped back and lowered his zipper. I took note of every move he made as he discarded each piece of clothing. It was quiet. There were no words spoken until he stood before me, naked and vulnerable. My eyes automatically lowered on his body. A smile played on my lips.

He stepped closer to me. He unclasped my bra and let it fall to the floor. I slid my underwear off.

I stepped towards the bed, pulled the covers down and slid myself between the sheets.

Tom switched off the overhead light and then turned on a night light next to the bed. A dim light illuminated him against the darkness when he joined me.

"Is the light okay? I can put the other one back on or turn them both off if you prefer?" Tom asked.

"Everything is fine as it is," I replied.

Like a blank canvas waiting to be painted on, my artist took his time exploring my body, giving me the chance to do the same with his. His gentleness only made me want him more. When he pulled his body into me, we came together as one. I didn't want to be anywhere else except under those sheets with Tom.

Perhaps this was what making love was like.

We lay side by side in each other's arms, catching our breaths. I didn't care where my clothes were or what time it was. This was what I needed tonight: to feel wanted, to feel special.

Tom kissed the top of my head. "I think this calls for ice cream," he said.

"I won't say no."

He got out of bed and pulled on a pair of boxers. I whistled at him before he disappeared out the door.

"Don't go anywhere, I'll be right back," he said, poking his head back inside.

I pulled the pillow from under my head and threw it toward him, but it fell short. His laughter faded down the hallway.

I lay naked under the covers, thinking about how different I felt with Tom. He and JD both had the same equipment, but Tom's gentleness, his thoughtfulness made the difference that set them apart. My heart ached just a little. Part of me felt like I was cheating on JD, but then again, JD was cheating on me, too.

Oh wait, I forgot. We broke up. I'm not cheating.

I blinked, erasing JD from my head.

Tom carried in two bowls of ice cream. I sat up and saw a mountain of ice cream in each bowl. A smile spread across my lips.

"Strawberry or chocolate?" he asked, lifting both bowls.

This was one decision I didn't mind having to make. I considered my choices and said, "Uhm, both."

Yes, I want both. I wasn't sure if I was only referring to ice cream, either.

Tom slid into bed next to me. "Great choice," he said, and we shared the bowls. Taking the last bite of ice cream, I looked over at the clock.

"Tom, it's 10:50," I said, jumping out of bed. "I have to be home at eleven."

"I wish you could stay longer. I don't want you to leave, but I don't want to get you in trouble."

While he drove me home, we chatted about the houses we passed, imagining the people who might live there. That lead to talking about what our own dream houses would look like. I thought about my house back home when I had parties and how the house would be lit up. I was sure there were no lights on now. But I couldn't picture what my dream house would be like. There were many times when my future had been hazy.

Tom pulled into the Bartlett's driveway. "I had a really nice time tonight. I hope you did, too."

"I did. It was nice. Dinner was delish and… "

Should I say it?

"I enjoyed *all* the dessert, too."

Tom laughed. I initiated the kiss this time, exploring his familiar mouth. I pulled away, planted a final kiss on his lips, and opened the car door.

"I'll give you a call tomorrow, and we'll plan something. I want to take advantage of the time you have off from school this week. Now, get going before I pull you back in here," Tom said.

"Good night, Tom."

He blew a kiss my way.

Tom and I spent the rest of the week together riding horses at his ranch, going to movies, and hanging out at his house (which translated to eating, drinking, and screwing). By the end of the week, I was exhausted. I'd never had such a great spring break, and I couldn't believe it was with someone I didn't even know very well. Was it possible to fall in love with someone in only a few days, or was I falling in love with sex? And was it okay to fall in love with sex? Because I wasn't sure I was ready to fall in love…again.

* * *

A week later, I called Holly. The phone rang three times.

"Hey, Holly, did you get my message?"

"Yeah, but when I called, the number wasn't in service anymore."

"Oh yeah, I'd probably moved already."

"So, where are you living now?" Holly asked.

"I'm living with my guidance counselor and her husband."

"Ah, everything cool with that?"

"Yeah, I really didn't have a choice. The Bartlett's are great people. The only problem is I can't come and go like I used to, and no boys are allowed in their house, but it's only for a few more months."

"That sucks, but sometimes you gotta do what you gotta do. So, what's new in the bedroom?"

"Ha, only you would ask this. Well, gosh, I haven't talked to you for a while, have I? First, JD broke up with me right before spring break a week ago."

"What?"

"Yep, he said he needed his space," I said.

"What a dick."

"Yeah. Maybe I should call his best friend Jason and ask him why JD really broke up with me."

"I'm sure he won't tell you—you know the bro-code guys have."

"Yeah, you're probably right. But then I met this other hottie."

"Ooh, tell me more," she said.

"His name is Tom. He's a couple years older, and He lives on a ranch, his ranch. I've been spending a lot of time with him. And, well, I kind of slept with him…"

"Shut your mouth. You didn't?"

"Yep, it was so nice. I mean, he was so different than JD."

"Yeah, guys all have the same tool, but they all do it differently."

"Thanks for your insight," I said.

"Anytime. Got yourself a cowboy, huh?"

"Yeah, I guess I do. How are you and Rusty doing?"

"Still good, I can't complain. You know what Rusty's like. He'll never change."

"I'm happy for you. You'll always know what you have with him."

"Yep."

"Hey, Holly, this might be a weird thing to say, but do you ever feel like we're living a real-life Cinderella story or a Snow-White movie?"

"What are you talking about?"

"I'm not sure, but it seems like every fairy tale has some guy who comes along and rescues the girl and takes her away. First, there's Prince Charming, who rides up on a white horse and kisses Snow White and brings her back to life, and they ride off together happily ever after. And then a prince brings Cinderella the glass slipper she lost running back to her wretched life, and he carries her away. I'm thinking it might have something to do with shoes. Anyway, these stories make it sound like we need a man to rescue us and then live happily ever after."

"You're right. But I hope we don't need a man to rescue us and then form us into what they want us to be," She said.

"I know. I don't want to have to rely on some guy to make me happy. I want to find happiness on my own," I said.

"You can say that again."

"Yep, or maybe I need to go shoe shopping and forget about men for a while."

"Ha… Well, remember, girlfriend, if the glass slipper breaks, you're going to get cut. So carry Band-aids."

"Thanks. You're right. The last thing I want to do is get hurt again. I gotta go."

"Remember, there's no place like home, so come back and visit me. It's not the same without you."

"I know. I will. Holly, how come every time we talk, I do all the talking?"

"Because your life is more interesting."

"I'm not sure I'd say that. Talk to you later, Holly."

Seventeen

Capricorns have zero tolerance when it comes to being made fun of

Sunday, I was at the grocery store picking out avocados for my famous guacamole when I heard a voice behind me.

"I see you got the JD spring break treatment."

Jessica stood next to me. Her blonde hair was in a ponytail. She wore bright pink lipstick and a smug expression.

"I'm not sure what you mean, *Jessica*," I said.

"Oh, I'm sure you do. You know, the 'I need my space' BS right before he goes to Cabo," she said.

I said nothing, glaring at her and hating her pink lips.

"He did the same thing to me last year."

I stepped away, but she followed.

"Here's what he does. His family goes to Cabo every year with his dad's law partner and family They have a daughter named… I believe it's Cassie. I'm not sure, and it doesn't matter anyway. She's our age, and she goes to school at Valley Christian. So, every year, JD hooks up with her. But he has to break up with whoever he's going out with right before he leaves so he can fool around and not feel like he's cheating."

"Yeah, Jessica, I guess I *did* get the JD treatment," I said.

"I'm sure you hate having to hear this from *me,* don't you." She smirked.

I bet she loved rubbing this in my face.

"At least I'm not stupid enough to go back to him after what he did."

A frown darkened her face as she slithered away.

"Bitch," I muttered under my breath.

* * *

Almost a week after Karen and I talked about my mom and her Dear Abby letter, I decided I needed to do something I should have done a long time ago. I opened my notebook and stared blankly at the blue-lined paper. The beginning was easy:

> Dear Mom,
>
> I want to let you know what has been happening since you left. I'm living with my guidance counselor, Karen, and her husband, Dan, my tennis coach. (Perhaps you recall telling the principal I would play tennis so you wouldn't have to pay for school?) Anyway, they have been very good to me, and I am happy living here. They make sure I do my homework (all of it), and they challenge me to do better. We talk about what I want to do and should do after I graduate. They tell me I can be anything I want to be - they actually talk to me when I need someone to talk too, and they never push me away. They never make me feel like I'm a burden, and they smile. They're happy people.
>
> Did you ever do any of this? (I'll answer for you—no.)

I stopped writing for a minute and leaned back, resting on my pillow. I counted the number of pages I had left in my notebook. I didn't have enough paper to write about all the bad things she'd said and done to me. I had to pick the ones that hurt the most.

> I want you to know I think about you every night when I go to bed, just as I always have my entire life. I know I've never told you this, but when I was younger, and you were gone for the weekend, I wondered if you would come back. I felt so alone. My heart broke every night. I also thought about you dying and what would happen to me, especially when I found four large garbage bags of marijuana in the back of your closet. You probably didn't know I found them— but I did. I worried about what would have happened if the police found out and what would happen to you or me? I was afraid they would take me away. And then I wondered if they did take me away or if I died would you even care or miss me?
>
> I have a lot of time to think about my life. And I wonder why you couldn't see how much I wanted to be loved, since you wanted to be loved too, or was I not the one who you wanted to love you? I can't help but wonder if the pot ruined you and our life. I still wonder if there is a way I could fix you and make you happy. But you aren't here. I am, so I'm going to fix myself.
>
> I have two more questions. How could you drive away and leave me standing in an empty parking lot? I guess it doesn't matter much anymore. Even though you left me alone on the pavement that afternoon, I am not alone anymore, so don't worry about me. I didn't leave you. YOU left me.
>
> Last thing I wanted to tell you is no matter how much BS and heartache has come my way, I never ran... I NEVER RAN AWAY. WHY DID YOU?

This letter was way longer than I wanted to write, but I had to get everything off my chest. I blotted the teardrops that had fallen on the paper and ended it there. I pulled that page out and started another letter:

> Dear Dad,
> I want to let you know I'm okay. I...

Someone knocked on my door.

"Phone, Sandy," Karen said.

Thinking it was Tom calling, I pushed the unfinished letter away and picked up the phone.

"Hey, I was just thinking about you," I said.

"Ah, really? I'm glad," said JD.

"Ah, JD… no." I sat up quickly.

I should hang up right now. He doesn't deserve my time.

But maybe I need to get this off my chest too.

I'm going to make him wish he never called me tonight.

Don't swear, don't swear. I had to watch my language.

Karen and Dan had told me I said the F word too much. Take a deep breath, and talk with a smile on your face, that will help to not swear.

"Actually, JD, I wasn't thinking about you at all," I said.

"Oh, Uhm, can we talk?"

"No, I think maybe you still need some more space. I know I do."

"Sandy, don't be like this," he begged.

"I don't think there's anything to talk about, JD. Besides, I'm seeing someone." I paced back and forth between my bed and my dresser.

"What? Who?" JD asked.

"Ah, I'm not sure if you know him," I said.

"Who? Who are you going out with?" he asked sharply.

I picked up a photo of Tom and me at the rodeo. "Do you know Tom Carrillo?" I asked.

"What? Carrillo? You're not serious…"

"Why wouldn't I be?"

"Since when?" he asked.

"Uhm, since you 'needed your space' and went to Cabo. I found I needed my space too."

"Sandy, please tell me you're not going out with him."

I took a deep breath in front of the mirror. I pushed my shoulders back and held my head up.

"I am, and I have been all last week— every day and night." I held my breath and waited for him to respond.

"Sandy, what do I have to do to get you back?" he asked.

"Are you groveling, JD? I didn't think players groveled for anything."

"I told you I'm not a player," he said.

"Yet you played me, didn't you?"

"I guess I thought if we broke up, I wouldn't be cheating on you—or 'playing you,' if you want to call it that—I guess I was wrong."

"I guess you found out the hard way. You thought I was stupid. I'm not some toy you take off a shelf to play with and discard when you're done."

"I know. I know I was an ass for what I did to you. And I don't think you're stupid. I was stupid, and you proved to me just how stupid I was. Give me another chance? I'll prove to you I'm not the player you think. I guess I thought I could be a player… but then I found myself completely in love."

"JD…"

"Can you please dump Carrillo and come back to me? Please?" He begged.

"Are you kidding me?" I opened my bedroom door and peeked down the hallway to see if anyone was listening. "Now you want me back? What about your space, JD, and what about what's her name?" I sat down on my bed. My stomach quivered.

"Cassie meant nothing to me…"

"I don't care what her name is, and I don't care how much she does or doesn't mean to you. You should have thought about this before you told me you needed your space. Or should I say, how you wanted to screw around with her and not have me find out."

"How do you know about her?" JD asked.

"Does *Jessica* ring a bell? I had a really nice talk with her today at the grocery store." I picked up the letters I'd written to my parents. "She seemed to know all about Cassie and you needing your space right before spring break."

"Sandy, I—"

"Goodbye, JD."

Letters clutched in my shaking hand, I tore them in half and then into a million pieces. I watched the million little pieces of my life fall and scatter on the floor.

I couldn't believe JD did this. Dan was right and so was Jessica.

JD was such a dog.

I tried holding my shoulders back and lifting my chin, but my heart kept pulling it down. Why did I let JD get to me?

The next day at school, JD was waiting for me at my locker. "Hey, Sandy."

"Why are you here? Don't you have your own locker to go to?"

"Are you really going out with Tom?" he asked, watching me spin the dial on my locker.

"Yes! Now leave me alone." I grabbed my books, slammed the door, and left him standing at my locker. A few feet away, I looked back to see if he was still there. He was, but he didn't see me look back.

Tom and I have been dating for a couple of weeks. He took me out to dinner at a swanky restaurant. The menu was limited to a few specialized entrées. I guess if I was going to continue dating him, I needed to broaden my horizons when it came to eating. After we ordered, Tom took both my hands in his from across the table. "I have to go to Durango to work the ranch."

"When?"

"I leave in two weeks," he said.

"When will you be back?"

"I guess we need to talk about this. I have to live on the ranch full-time," he answered, lowering his voice.

"What do you mean? What about your flight school? Why do you have to leave so soon?"

"My parents need me in Durango as soon as possible." He hesitated. "And I'll finish my flight classes there."

I pushed back in my chair and pulled my hands away from his. My heart pounded. I had to blink several times to prevent tears from escaping. "So, we're breaking up?"

"No, we're not breaking up. I'm letting you know where I'm going and what I'm doing," he said.

"I don't understand what you're saying. You're leaving, and I'm staying. How do you think this is going to work?" I asked.

"I was hoping I could fly you down to Durango on Friday nights, then fly you back on Sundays."

"That's not going to work, Tom. First, Karen and Dan would never allow that. Second, I don't want a weekend boyfriend."

He reached over to retake my hands. I backed away.

"Let's not talk about this here," he said quietly.

"How long have you known you were going to be leaving?"

"A while, I guess," he said sheepishly.

"Before we met?"

"Yeah," he slowly admitted. "But…"

"Why did you even ask me out then? Why are we here? You should have told me earlier," I said, betrayed.

"I wanted to, but I didn't think you'd go out with me then," he said.

"Yeah, you're right. I probably wouldn't have. I guess I thought there was more to our relationship."

The waiter brought our food and set my plate in front of me. I pushed it away. "I'm not hungry anymore," I said.

"Sandy, please eat."

"Don't tell me what to do, Tom."

"I didn't mean it like that. I want you to eat—I want you to at least enjoy your dinner."

I pushed the food around on the plate with my fork. My stomach was in knots. I couldn't believe Tom was leaving just like my mom and JD.

Why does everyone leave me? What am I doing wrong?

Why can't I make people stay?

I clutched both sides of the table for support. "What is it about you guys anyway? First, JD broke up with me so he could screw around with some chick while he's on vacation. Then, you start a relationship with me, knowing you're going to leave in a month and think I'm going to fly all over the place and be a weekend girlfriend?"

"Please lower your voice a little," he said.

"Are you telling me to be quiet?"

"So, that's why you and JD broke up?" Tom asked.

He just ignored my question. I pushed myself away from the table. "What? We're not talking about him right now. This is about you and me." I jabbed my finger toward him. "Take me home… now!"

"I think you're getting a little emotional…"

"What did you just say?"

"Ah, nothing. Forget it." He wiped his mouth with his napkin. "Let's go."

Neither one of us said anything on the drive home. He pulled into the driveway and put his truck in park. "Sandy, think about it for—"

I closed my eyes hoping to push Tom out of my head. I wanted him gone, I didn't want to hurt anymore. "No, I'm done thinking about it, Tom. It's not going to work. I can't leave with you. I'm not where you are in life. I don't know who I am right now. I need to figure out what's important and what's not. It's not you. It's me."

"I totally understand why you're mad. I should have told you earlier. You're a nice girl. I didn't mean to hurt you. I wish it didn't have to be over between us, but I understand you can't come on the weekends. It probably wouldn't work out anyway."

As I listened to him, my eyes started to water. I closed my eyes and squeezed them tight so I wouldn't cry. I didn't want to hear any more. I got out of his car, but before I closed the door, Tom said, "I'm sorry."

I closed the door and watched him drive away. Every minute we spent together flashed through my mind. I wondered what I was letting get away.

Before I went inside, I sat on the porch. I overreacted tonight when Tom told me he was leaving. I wanted to run and hide. I wanted to build a wall around me so he couldn't hurt me, and then, I pushed him away with my words. Did I just let something good get away?

When I opened the front door, Karen was sitting at the kitchen table, going through paperwork. I closed the door behind me and sank to the floor.

"What's wrong?" she asked.

I covered my eyes. "I hate my life."

"Come over here and tell me what happened."

I crawled to the table and sat next to her. "I don't even know what happened. I mean, we're going out, having fun, and the next thing I know, he's leaving town."

"Tom's… leaving town? Why?"

"He's going to his family's ranch in Durango to work."

"Oh, I'm sorry, Sandy."

"I'm never going out with anyone ever again." I got up.

"Before you go, here's a copy of my Dear Abby letter. I thought you might want it."

I took it from her and hugged her. "Thanks, Karen."

I climbed in bed and pulled the blankets over my head. I had nobody to dream about: no Tom, no JD. I closed my eyes and tried to forget about tonight. JD crept into my head. Should I take him back? Did he really want me back? Did I only want to go back to him to forget Tom? And did I only go out with Tom to forget JD? Was I a pawn in their game? Was being with someone better than being alone? My heart hurt. Love sucked.

EIGHTEEN

Capricorns blossom when the struggle is the hardest

Yesterday was bad. Today, I'm going to fix it.

NINETEEN

Capricorns want to make things better in the real world

A few days later, Holly called. I missed talking to her every day. Sometimes, just hanging out with your bestie was enough to forget your troubles.

"Hey, Holly, how's it going?"

"Good. What's new with you?"

"Man, I swear to God I could write a book about my life right now."

"So, tell your therapist all about it," she said.

"Ha, you crack me up."

"That's what I'm here for."

"Yeah, you always have been. Where did I leave off during our last call?"

"You were telling me about Hottie Number Two - Cowboy Tom. Was that his name?"

"Haha, yeah. Well, we broke up," I said.

"What? Why?"

"I had to let him go. We were going in different directions."

"Now what?"

"I'm going to hang up my cowboy hat and boots for now," I said.

"I'm sure that wasn't a good look on you, anyway."

"Yeah, I hated the hat hair. JD has been calling me. He wants me to go back out with him."

"Don't tell me you went back to him. You've never given *anyone* a second chance before."

"I know, but part of me wants him back, and part of me doesn't. He's got a hold over me somehow. I keep thinking about everything we've been through. He was there for me with all the bullshit I went through with my mom since I've been out here. But I'm still mad at him for what he did to me on spring break."

"Never let a good girl go because it will kill you when you watch her be great to another man," Holly said.

"Oh, I like that. Someone should put that on a bumper sticker."

"Someone already did. I saw it a few days ago."

"And now, JD wants to know everything I did with Tom."

"Don't tell him anything. He doesn't need to know. Besides, did he tell you what he did with sidepiece Cabo girl?"

"No, and I don't want to know either," I said.

"Wouldn't it be funny if it was 'that time of the month' and he didn't get anything?"

"Oh my god, you're so funny. Thanks for making me laugh."

"Again, that's what I'm here for. I've gotta go. Rusty just pulled up. I'll talk to you later, goofball."

"Yeah, talk to you later, Holly."

"Oh, one more thing."

"What?"

"Whether you take JD back or not, you're going to be okay."

"I know."

I pulled out a framed photo of JD that was buried in my nightstand and stared at it for a long time—my heart hurt. I held it against my chest and then put it back face down in the drawer and closed it.

* * *

Tennis started. I was off to a good start, winning most of my matches, but I was losing matches, too. The ones I lost weighed on me the most. I wanted those moments back so I could change the outcome. I thought slamming the ball as hard as I could at my opponent would ensure me a win. I didn't want anyone having an advantage over me. I needed to prove how good I was to my opponent—to everyone. Winning meant everything. Everyone loved a winner, and I wanted to be a winner.

"Sandy, I want you to try attacking the ball more aggressively," Dan said.

"I am hitting the ball hard."

"No, not hard. You don't need to kill the ball or kill your opponent with your 'I want to kill you' face. You need to control the ball. You do that by controlling your actions, and by controlling your actions, you will ultimately control your opponent's actions."

My eyes glazed over.

I don't need a lecture about my life right now, Dan.

"You told me you use to hit a tennis ball against the basement wall, right?"

"Yeah."

"What did you focus on when you hit the ball?"

"I don't know."

"Yes, you do. Think about it. You had to focus on hitting the wall and not hitting a window or a door, right?"

"Yeah."

"That's controlling the ball and your actions. Focus on where you want the ball to go by controlling your actions."

"I wish it was that easy," I said.

"You can achieve everything you want to in time with hard work and patience. Life is like this, too. You have to focus on where you want to go in life. Either you stand or you fall. Let's go home," Dan said.

I tossed my racket in the back seat and got in the front.

"So, I guess you don't get to go to any of JD's baseball games, do you?" Dan asked.

"No, I don't. If I have a home match, he has an away game. But that's okay, I don't want him to watch me play either."

"Why not?"

"I don't know. I guess I don't want him to see me lose."

"That's stupid. You can't win all the time," he said.

"But I want to win. If I don't win, I feel like I've failed. I don't want to be a failure."

"Losing doesn't make you a failure—not trying at all makes you a failure."

"Part of me thinks if I do everything right, then people will like me, and the other part of me says 'F' it, because I really don't care what others think."

"I would go with the second part. 'F' it. And don't tell Karen I said that."

"Nice, Dan…I mean, Coach Dan.

Dan looked over at me. "I can tell there's something else on your mind—What's wrong?"

"Can we not go home yet?" I asked

Dan pulled into a forest preserve and parked.

I closed my eyes and sucked in my stomach. "I don't think I want to go back out with JD."

"How about taking it slow with JD?"

"No."

"Okay, but what made you change your mind?"

"I want to stay away from people who have hurt me."

"That's not a bad idea. But people do change."

"Not the people I know." I hesitated for a moment. "I saw Tom at my match yesterday."

"I saw him too. I wasn't sure if you saw him or not."

"Dan, how do you know what you're supposed to do…I mean, how do you know what boys are good for you?"

"You are way too young to settle down with one guy. Don't worry about boys now. Just focus on yourself, where you want to go in life and what *you* want to do. Boys will come later."

"So, you're just supposed to figure everything out on your own?"

"Yep. There's no guide book for what you should do. You learn about life through trial and error." He touched my shoulder. "You're going to be okay."

"Yeah, I'm going to be okay."

"Let's go home. Oh, and before I forget I have one more thing to talk to you about."

"What now?" I asked.

"Mrs. Adams wants you to give a speech at graduation."

"Why me? What could I possibly say that anyone would want to hear?"

"Oh, I'm sure you'll have a lot to talk about. You can start with how far you've come since you moved here. I'll help you with it. You can also tell everyone what a great tennis coach you have, too."

* * *

June 1980

On graduation day, everyone was in their assigned seats in the gymnasium waiting for the ceremony to start. Mrs. Adams began with the usual opening address, and then the valedictorian gave her commencement speech. It was funny how they always said the same thing: "Work hard, go far, and don't forget where you came from." At least, that's what I thought she said.

"Let's be real here. Try walking in my shoes, even for one day. I bet you couldn't," I said under my breath.

When it was my turn, I stood at the lectern. My hands were sweaty and shaking.

"I always believed the only people who gave speeches were the smart ones, the straight-A students. I'm not one of those people. I've come a long way since moving here last fall. Most of you don't know my story. I moved here from Chicago at the start of my senior year, having to leave many friends and some family behind to start a new life."

I paused for a second as emotions welled up inside me. "Life at home was not easy for me." I took a deep breath and continued. "I had many challenges to overcome and choices to make that would, and will, forever change and shape my life.

"What have I learned? For one, life was full of challenges, changes, and decisions we have to make along the way," I said. My upper lip started quivering. "Never be afraid to make mistakes, for this is how we learn. Never be afraid of change." A tear escaped and ran down my face. " Be ready to change direction at any time. Never be afraid to let go and walk away, even when you don't think you can. Put one foot in front of the other, and move forward. Keep moving. You'll be amazed at how far you can go. Never be afraid to travel a different path than others. Some of the roads you need to take may have detours. Not all roads will lead where you want to go, but they will take you somewhere. Stay focused. Stay in control, and don't let yourself be controlled.

"Welcome a challenge, and find ways around the roadblocks that come your way. Always, always have a Plan B and, most importantly, never be afraid to open your heart and love again.

"After today, we will all go in different directions. Some of you will go off to college or move away. Many will join the workforce here in town, and a few will join the military to fight for our freedom."

"For those of you going to college," I looked over at JD. My heart ached a little. "I wish you luck with all the hard work that awaits you." I found Tammy a few rows back. "And for those of you staying around town to find work locally, good luck with your new jobs and future, and I hope to run into you... and for those of you who will be joining the military," my voice cracked. I pointed at Jamison. He nodded. "I will pray for you and your safety. For tomorrow, you will be our heroes." I paused, wiping away my tears with a shaking hand. I swallowed hard and took a deep breath. I saw Tom standing in the back. My heart leaped.

And for those who have to ride off into the sunset to Durango, I'll never forget you.

I rested my hand on my stomach.

"Stay hungry. This is where the strength to move forward will come from. I'm done. I have nothing more to say except… peace." I raised my hand and flashed a peace sign. My classmates responded by raising their hands with peace signs, too.

The next day, I was in my room packing. A horn honked outside.

"Sandy, your ride is here," Karen shouted down the hall.

"I'm coming." Before I closed my bedroom door, I looked around the room one last time.

"I'm leaving now, Karen and Dan."

They both wrapped their arms around me.

"Have fun, but not too much fun. And don't forget your Cosmetology class starts in August," Karen said.

"I won't forget."

"Be safe. And call us if you need anything," Dan said.

"I'll be fine."

The horn blew again.

"I gotta go."

Karen had tears in her eyes. "Goodbye, Katniss."

I smiled back at her and blew her a kiss.

I threw my suitcase in the back seat and jumped in the front. "Where too, Bestie?"

"I don't know yet. Which direction should we go?" Holly asked.

"West…lets go West," I said.

Sometimes you meet a girl
She becomes your best friend
No matter the distance
No matter the time between the last time you saw her
She is still your best friend forever.

TWENTY

Capricorns are loyal

I didn't go to my mother's funeral. My sister, *in blood only,* uninvited me by changing the date so I would miss it, and that was okay.

* * *

February 11, 2013

"Tell me about your mother. What kind of mother was she?" asked the hospice nurse.

My mother's pail, motionless body, lay before me, her lips spread as the oxygen mask forced air into her cancer-filled lungs.

"If that were me or my sister lying in that bed, I don't think she would be here."

Her warm hand covered mine. "I'm sorry."

"Don't be sorry. I'm not sure if I'm here for her or me."

"It doesn't matter. You're here. Tell me your story. I want to understand the woman I'll be taking care of for the last few days of her life."

I thought for a few minutes. "If I wrote a book about my life, this is how it would start. I grew up in Chicago. I found love in Breckenridge. I died every day in my mother's life until I found myself in the West, and I never went hungry."

"I'm listening," she said.

THE END

When is the last time you reached out to that friend, the one you haven't seen in days, months, years that means the world to you?

Made in the USA
Las Vegas, NV
16 February 2021